THE LUCKY
BASEBALL BAT

With Illustrations by
ROBERT HENNEBERGER

THE LUCKY
BASEBALL
BAT

by Matt Christopher

LITTLE, BROWN AND COMPANY
New York   Boston

To
Marty, Pam, and Dale

Copyright © 1954 by Matt Christopher Royalties, Inc.

Little, Brown and Company

Hachette Book Group
1290 Avenue of the Americas, New York, NY 10104
Visit our website at lb-kids.com

mattchristopher.com

Little, Brown and Company is a division of Hachette Book Group, Inc.
The Little, Brown name and logo are trademarks of Hachette Book Group, Inc.

The publisher is not responsible for websites (or their content) that are not owned by the publisher.

First Anniversary Edition: August 2004
First published in hardcover in 1954 by Little, Brown and Company

Matt Christopher® is a registered trademark of Matt Christopher Royalties, Inc.

Library of Congress Control Number: 54-5141

ISBN: 978-0-316-01012-2

20 19

LSC - C

Printed in the United States of America

THE LUCKY
BASEBALL BAT

I

MARVIN bit his lip and mopped his damp forehead with a grimy handkerchief. His sister Jeannie, two years younger than he, scowled at him.

"What're you afraid of? Go in there and ask them."

"Ask who?" Marvin said.

He looked from her to the group of boys scattered on the ball field. They were practicing, just throwing the ball among themselves to limber up their muscles and get the feel of it. The sun was shining through a thin layer of cloud, with a lot of blue sky around it. Many of the boys wore short-sleeved jerseys.

Jeannie brushed a tangle of curly hair away from her eyes and pointed. "Ask that man there. Jim Cassell. He's the captain or something, isn't he?"

Marvin didn't like to go and ask Jim Cassell. Jim might tell him to go home. He didn't know Marvin, and Marvin didn't know him. That was the trouble. Marvin hardly knew anybody here. They had just moved into the city.

"I think I'll just go out there with those kids and see if they'll throw a ball to me," he said after thinking for a

while. "That'll be all right, won't it?"

Jeannie nodded. "Go ahead. Maybe it's the best way, anyway."

Marvin felt pleased because he had figured that one out without anybody's help. He started out at a slow run toward the scattered group of boys. They were all about his size, some a little smaller, some taller. Most of them had baseball gloves. He wished he had one. You didn't look like a baseball player without a baseball glove.

All at once he heard Jim Cassell's voice shout out to them. "Okay, boys! Spread out! A couple of you get in center field!"

The boys scampered into position. Marvin didn't move. Jim Cassell was

6

having the boys start batting practice. A tall, skinny kid stood on the mound. He pitched the ball twice. Each time the boy at bat swung at the ball and missed.

The third time he connected. Marvin heard the sharp crack! It was followed by a scramble of feet not far behind him. He looked up and sure enough the ball, like a small white pill, was curving through the air in his direction!

"I got it! I got it!" he cried. He forgot that he had no glove. His sneakers slipped on the short-cut grass as he tried to get in position under the ball.

Somebody bumped into him, but he didn't give ground. "I got it!" he yelled again.

The ball came directly at him and he reached for it with both hands. The next instant it changed to a blur and he felt it slide through his hands and strike solidly against his chest.

His heart sank. Missed it!

"Nice catch!" a boy sneered. "Where did you learn how to play ball?"

Marvin gave him a cold look and shut his lips tight to keep his anger from spilling out. Another boy who had come running over stopped and threw darts with his eyes too.

"Who do you think you are, trying to catch a ball without a glove? Next time leave it alone," he said.

Marvin looked at his bare hands, feeling his heart pound in his chest. He walked away, sticking his hands into his pockets. He could feel the hot sun burning his neck.

"Kid!" Jim Cassell's voice yelled from across the field. "Hey, son!"

Marvin turned.

"For Petey sakes," Jim said, "don't try to catch a ball without a glove! You'll get hurt!"

Marvin looked away, his lips still pressed tight together. "Come on," he said to Jeannie. "Let's go home."

"Sure," Jeannie replied in disgust. "You can do something else besides play baseball with those boys."

"But I don't want to do anything else!" Marvin said, angrily. "I want to play baseball!"

9

Then he looked up. A tall, dark-haired boy was watching him — a boy of high-school size, with broad shoulders. He seemed to be amused about something.

2

HELLO," said the high-school boy. "What's the matter, fella? You look as if you'd lost your best friend!"

Marvin tried to smile, just to show that he wasn't mad at everybody. "Nothing's the matter," he answered, his eyes on the ground. He kept walking with his hands in his pockets, his heels scraping the dirt and pebbles. Jeannie had hold of his arm, as if whatever suffering he was going through she was going through with him.

"Hey, wait a minute!" the tall stranger called after them as they started by. He caught Marvin's arm in his big fist and Marvin had to stop. The smile on the stranger's face turned into a bigger one. "You didn't answer me. What happened? Won't they let you play ball with them?"

"I haven't got a glove," Marvin said. "I'm sure I could catch those balls if I had a glove."

The tall boy laughed. Marvin liked the sound and turned to look at Jeannie to see what she was thinking. Her blue eyes were crinkling in a cheerful grin, and Marvin knew she felt the same way he did. Whoever this tall boy was, he was nice.

"Tell you what," the stranger said. "My name's Barry Welton. I live about two blocks around the corner on Grant Street, to the right."

"We live a block to the left," Jeannie said warmly. "I'm Jeannie Allan, and this is my brother Marvin."

"Well! That's fine!" He made a motion with his hand. "Come on," he said, and began to walk toward Grant Street.

"Where you going?" Marvin asked, wondering.

"To my house. I'm going to give you something. Something I think you'll like to have."

When they reached his house, a gray wooden frame building with yellow shutters, he asked them to wait in the living room while he ran upstairs. He came back down a couple of seconds later, and Marvin's eyes almost bugged from his head.

Barry was carrying a bat and a glove!

"Here," he grinned. "These are yours. Now maybe they'll let you play. Okay?"

"Christmas!" Marvin cried. "You mean you're giving these things to me?"

"Certainly! I've had that glove ever since I was your size, and I outgrew that bat years ago. It was a lucky bat for me. Maybe it'll be a lucky one for you, too."

"Christmas!" said Marvin again, his heart thumping excitedly. "Thanks! Thanks a lot, Barry!"

He could not make up his mind whether to return to the ball diamond or not. Those boys had not liked it because he had butted in on them by trying to catch a ball without a glove. But he had a glove now. They shouldn't say anything.

"Come on, Jeannie. Let's go back to the park," he said.

She looked at him strangely, then together they walked back to the ball field.

Marvin saw that they were still having batting practice. He let Jeannie hang on to the bat while he put on the glove and ran out to the field. Two of the boys saw him with his glove, and said something to each other. He acted as if he didn't see them. He didn't care what they said. He had as much right here as the rest of them.

Suddenly he saw Jim Cassell gazing toward the outfield. Jim seemed to be looking directly at him, and Marvin's heart fell.

"Kid!" Jim yelled then, motioning with his hand. "Move over a little — toward center field!"

A thrill of excitement went through him. Jim Cassell had given him an order as if he were already a member of the team!

He ran over to a spot between left and center fields. He almost prayed a ball would come his way. He had not caught a ball since last summer, but he knew how to do it. Maybe he could even show them something!

And then, even while he was thinking about it, he saw a ball hit out his way. The closer of the two boys Jim Cassell had placed in center field came running for it, shouting at the top of his lungs, "I've got it! I've got it!"

Marvin knew it was his ball more than the other boy's. He needed only to take four or five steps backward. He reached up, trying to make his yell sound out above the other's.

"It's mine! Let it go! It's mine!"

"Let him take it, Tommy!" Jim Cassell's voice boomed from near home plate.

Marvin felt a shoulder hit his arm. It threw him off balance enough so that the ball struck the fingers of his glove and slipped right through. Bang! On his chest again, barely missing his throat. The ball dropped to the grass and bounced away.

Marvin turned, tears choking him. It was the same boy who had earlier made a nasty remark to him.

"So it's you again," the boy said. "With a glove, too!" He laughed. "Even with a glove you miss them. Why don't you go home and stay there? We don't want any farmers on this team!"

3

THIS time when Marvin and Jeannie went home there was no
Barry Welton around. Marvin was glad
Barry had not seen how foolish he
looked on the diamond.

"I'm glad you came home, chil-
dren," their mother said, as she saw
them coming through the hall into the
kitchen. "We're almost ready for supper."

Then she caught sight of the bat and

glove Marvin was carrying. Her mouth made an oval. "Where on earth did you get those things?" she cried.

"A big boy by the name of Barry Welton gave them to me," Marvin said, and told his mother what had happened. She seemed surprised, but quite happy about Barry Welton's gift to Marvin.

The cellar door opened and Marvin's tall, husky father came in and stared at the bat and glove, too. Marvin had to tell all about it again. He left out one thing, though. He didn't tell them he was going to give the bat and glove back to Barry.

He did not feel like eating much for supper, but once he started his appetite improved. He had another helping and almost finished it before he caught his mother looking at him strangely. He slowed up but it was too late.

"Marvin, what's your hurry?"

"I'm sorry, Mother," he said. He didn't want to tell her he had baseball on his mind.

Marvin went outside after supper, and sat on the front porch in the shade. He expected Jeannie as soon as she finished helping Mother with the dishes. For a minute he got to thinking about Jeannie. If she had been a boy everything would have been all right. They could play baseball together, and get a lot of practice, and chum around like real pals. You can't do those things with a sister, he thought, even though Jeannie tried to be like a boy with him.

He didn't know how long he sat out there thinking. But all at once he heard leather heels clicking on the sidewalk. They were coming from down the street, and even before he looked to see who was making the sound, he knew who it was. It was Barry Welton.

"Hi, Barry!" he greeted when Barry got closer. It was hard to smile.

"Hi, Marv," Barry answered. "Taking it easy?"

Marvin nodded. "Wait a minute, Barry," he said, and went into the house. "I'll be right back."

He got the bat and glove and brought them out. "Here," he said, swallowing a lump in his throat. "Take them back,

Barry. They'll never let me play baseball around here!"

Barry frowned, then a grin came over his face. "Shucks, now, pal. Don't go acting like that or you'll never play ball! Have you got a ball?"

"In the house," Marvin said, wondering what Barry was driving at.

"Get it. We'll play a little catch."

Marvin ran into the house, full of excitement. The ball was in the closet where he kept all his things. He brought it out and tossed it to Barry.

"Let's go out to the side of the house," Barry said, "so that we won't be throwing toward the windows. You get over there and I'll have my back toward the street. Just make sure you

don't throw any wide balls!" he
laughed.

"I'll try not to," Marvin said, and
they started throwing the ball back and

forth between them, Marvin using the glove, and Barry barehanded. Marvin thrilled at the expert way Barry was catching the balls, pulling his hands down and away with the ball. He tried to do the same. Only, with the glove, he didn't have to do it so much.

They played about fifteen minutes, then Barry said he had to move along. He'd see Marvin tomorrow. In the meantime Jeannie had come out to sit on the porch, watching them. After Barry left, Marvin still wanted to play.

"Jeannie," he said, "how about throwing the ball to me in the back yard? I'll bat. Then after a while you can bat."

"Okay!"

He knew she would be willing. She was a swell sister, even if she wasn't a boy!

Out in the back yard they had much more room. The lawn was bordered by a hedge on two sides. In the back two tall elms with branches spreading out like big, crooked arms would be some protection if a ball were hit that far.

But it was not as much fun as Marvin had hoped. Each time Jeannie threw the ball he swung, and missed. He didn't want to swing too hard, of course. He might hit it squarely, and send it beyond the trees into the neighbor's yard. He might even break a window. And that he couldn't risk.

So he swung only lightly. A couple

of times he ticked the ball, and in the beginning he joked with Jeannie.

"Quit throwing those curves!" he'd say.

She would laugh, knowing as well as he that she did not have the faintest idea how to throw a curve.

But then missing the ball four, five, six times in a row got under his skin. Sweat began to break out on his forehead. He was growing warm all over, and he knew it was because he was getting anxious and mad.

"Marvin," said Jeannie, "what's the matter? Can't you even hit it?"

He took one final, hard swing. If he had hit it, it would surely have sailed beyond the big elm trees. But he missed.

28

His bat swished through the air, almost making him lose his balance.

Angrily, he threw the bat to the ground, ran around to the porch, and into the house. He ran to his bedroom, fell on his bed, and no longer tried to stop the tears.

4

MARVIN heard the door open. He didn't look up. His face was buried in the pillow. He could feel and taste the salty wetness that had soaked into it. The door closed and he heard Jeannie's voice.

"Marv, don't cry."

He didn't say anything. But hearing Jeannie made him want to stop crying.

He felt her warm hand on his back, rubbing him gently. "Please, Marv. I don't like to hear you cry. If — if you keep on, I — I'll probably start crying, too."

He rolled over on his side and wiped the tears from his cheeks with his wrist. He hated to cry. He was big now. He was ashamed to be letting tears spill all over the place. He got up.

"You're nice, Jeannie," he murmured softly.

Jeannie smiled, and he thought she really was going to cry, too.

Then a voice called from the kitchen: "Jeannie! Marvin!"

They ran out to the kitchen. Their mother was in front of the mirror, brushing her hair with short, pulling strokes. She smiled at them, her brown eyes sparkling.

31

"Want to go to the movies?" she asked.

"Yes!" They said it almost together, their faces brightening up like Christmas-tree bulbs.

"Well," she said, "wash yourselves and get dressed!"

They washed and put on their best going-out clothes, while their daddy went to get the car from the garage. By the time they were ready he had the car at the curb, a new-looking, pea-green sedan. They all piled in and headed for the movie. Jeannie and Marvin sat in the back seat. They were both very happy, and not once did Marvin think about baseball.

The movie was a comedy. They

32

laughed all the way through it.

Then they talked about it on the way home. Marvin and Jeannie told and re-told some of the funniest scenes and laughed about them. It was what they did every time after they saw a movie.

After they were home and in the house awhile Marvin remembered the bat he had left outside. Quickly, he raced out the side door, onto the porch and down the steps to the back yard. The sun had gone down, but the half-moon that hung in the sky looked big and yellow, almost close enough to hang a hat on. It made the trees and the roofs of the houses stand out sharp and black. It helped him see whatever was on the ground.

Marvin searched in and around the spot where he was sure he had left the bat. But it was nowhere around.

The bat was gone!

5

MARVIN could not sleep half the night, thinking about the bat. He thought over and over again how he had missed Jeannie's pitch, gotten mad, and thrown down the bat. That was a foolish thing to do — he knew that now. He should not have gotten mad in the first place. He should not have thrown the bat aside like that. At least, he should have gone back out right away and brought it into the house.

He would not have minded so much if Barry Welton had not given him the bat. But Barry had — and now it was gone. Somebody must have stolen it. Baseball bats don't just walk away.

Finally he fell asleep. He dreamed about the movie. He was one of the actors. He saw that another actor had the bat. But when he went to ask for it the actor showed him empty hands.

The next morning after breakfast he went out to the back yard again, just to see if he might have missed the bat last night. It could have rolled behind one of Mother's rose bushes, or into the higher grass that grew close to the wire fence. But he did not find it. The bat had really disappeared.

He walked out front. The sun, shining over the rooftops, felt hot against his face. He thought about going to the park. Maybe it was too early. Maybe none of the boys would be down there yet. He could not get the thought of the bat out of his mind. What could have happened to it? Did somebody take it? But who? And how?

He walked up to the corner where Ferrin Street crossed Grant. Down the street he saw some boys playing with a tennis ball. He recognized one of them. It was Rick Savora, who lived in the brick tenement house. The porch of the tenement house sagged on one corner and some of its windows were cracked.

Rick was about eleven or twelve — bigger than Marvin. He stood with his legs spread apart and held a bat on his shoulder, waiting for another boy to pitch him the tennis ball. Way back was another boy, waiting to chase the ball in case Rick hit it.

Marvin stood on the corner and waited to see what Rick would do. Rick, he remembered, was one of the boys at the park yesterday. He looked as if he might be the best player of them all.

Suddenly Rick swung at the ball, hit it, and it went bounding down the street past the pitcher. Rick dropped the bat and started scooting around squares of cardboard which were used for bases.

Then Marvin noticed the bat. It had rolled a little way as Rick had thrown it, and then stopped. Marvin's heart pounded like mad. He started to walk down the street.

One of the boys saw him.

"Here comes that Allan kid!" he cried out.

Rick stood on second, his hands on his knees as if he were getting ready to run for third. When he heard the boy shout he rose and scowled at Marvin.

"What do you want around here?" he yelled.

Marvin didn't answer. He looked at Rick and then again at the bat. The more he looked at it the more it looked like the one Barry had given him.

The boys muttered in low tones
among themselves. One of them walked
off the street. Rick picked up the card–

board piece that was second base, tucked it under his arm, then picked up the bat. He walked off the street, too. The boy who played catcher followed him.

All three gave Marvin dirty looks and went up on the porch of the house, the boards squeaking under their weight.

Marvin stopped and watched them. A hurt look crept into his eyes and an ache filled his throat, wanting to turn into tears. He spun on his heel and headed for home. He walked a little way, then started running. For some reason he could not explain, he wanted to get away from there as fast as he could.

6

HE met Jeannie in front of the house, bouncing a rubber ball up and down on the sidewalk. She caught the ball and looked up at him in surprise.

"I was looking for you," she said.

"Rick Savora's got my bat!" Marvin exclaimed. "I just saw him take it into the house."

Jeannie's eyes widened. "Did you ask him for it?"

"No. I didn't have a chance. He and some other kids went into his house when they saw me coming down the street."

Jeannie's lips tightened. She made a face, and Marvin knew she was disgusted.

"Let's go to his house and ask him for that bat," she said.

"Suppose he won't give it to me?" Marvin asked.

"Then we'll tell Daddy about it."

Marvin shook his head. "No. I won't tell Daddy anything. I don't want him mixed up in this."

"Well, let's go anyway. If it's your bat he must have stolen it, and he must give it back. I don't like stealers."

Together they walked to Rick Savora's house. The wooden steps creaked as they climbed to the porch. Marvin knocked on the door.

A lady opened it. "Yes?" she said. She brushed a lock of dark hair away from her face, and looked curiously from Jeannie to Marvin.

"Is Rick here?" Marvin asked nervously.

"Just a minute," she said. She turned around and in a louder voice called, "Rick! Somebody to see you!"

In a minute Rick came to the door.

He scowled when he saw who his callers were.

Marvin swallowed. "You were playing with my baseball bat," he said. "I want it back."

"You're crazy!" Rick snapped. "I haven't got your bat!"

"Yes, you have. You were playing with it on the street just a little while ago. I saw it."

Rick's eyes blazed with anger, but Marvin didn't care. Rick had his bat and he wanted it back.

"Just a minute," Rick said. "I'll be right back!"

He turned away from the door. Marvin could hear his heavy footsteps as he walked back through the house. Pretty soon Rick returned. He had a small yellow bat with him.

"There! Is that your bat?"

Marvin looked at it closely. "No,"

he said. "But that isn't the one you were playing with."

"You're crazy!" Rick said again. "You must've been seeing things!"

He closed the door so hard the wood panels shook. Jeannie and Marvin turned and stared at each other. Neither one knew what to say, or what to do.

"Let's go home," Marvin said then. His voice was so weak he could hardly hear it himself. He led the way down the steps.

"He's lying," he said to Jeannie as they started up the street. His heart pounded hard now. "I know he's lying!"

7

IT was a little after dinnertime when a black car stopped in front of Marvin as he sat on the porch. The man in the car said, "Hey, sonny! Want to come to the park and play ball?"

Marvin recognized Jim Cassell, manager of the small boys' team. He got off the porch and walked slowly toward the car.

Then he saw that Jim had somebody with him. Rick Savora. Rick didn't look at him.

Marvin felt a tightening in his chest. "I — I don't think so," he said. "I don't think I want to play baseball."

"Why not?" Jim Cassell's blue eyes studied Marvin, as if he could not understand why any boy did not care to play baseball.

Marvin shrugged. He did not want to say that he didn't care to play because Rick was on the team. He could not tell Jim that Rick had stolen his bat, that Rick had lied when he said he had not stolen it. It would be pretty cheap to tell on Rick. Let Jim find out himself what kind of kid Rick was. He would find out soon enough. Maybe by then Marvin would have his bat back.

Jim flashed a smile. "Got a glove?"

Marvin nodded. "Yes."

"Get it. We're going to have a team in the Grasshoppers League, and since you're one of the boys in the neighborhood maybe we'll have room for you on the team. Rick told me about you yesterday."

Marvin looked at Rick, but still Rick

did not look at him. He turned again to Jim Cassell.

"A Grasshoppers League?" He frowned. "What's that?"

"A league we have here. There are six teams in it. Each team plays two games a week during the summer vacation. The winner gets a free banquet and goes to see a World Series game. It's something worth shooting for. Don't you think so?"

"Christmas!" Marvin's face brightened. "I'll say it is!"

Jim's smile broadened. "Now you want to come along?"

"You bet! Wait! I'll run in and get my glove!"

8

AT the field Jim Cassell had two of the tallest boys choose sides. Rick Savora chose for one side, and a red-haired boy named Lennie Moore chose for the other. Marvin was picked on Lennie's team. Then Jim Cassell flipped a nickel to see whose side would bat first. Rick guessed "Heads," and chose to bat last.

Jim Cassell told the boys what positions they were to play, then called off the hitters for Lennie's team. Marvin noticed that Rick was playing shortstop. He wondered what position Jim would let him play. He had never thought about playing in a league! And to have a chance to see a World Series game! What a wonderful thing that would be! Even Daddy had never seen a World Series game!

"Okay, Marvin! Your turn to bat!"

He sprang from the bench on which he was sitting with the rest of the boys, surprised that his name was called so soon. The second one!

He picked up one of the bats and went to the plate. His heart hammered. He got into position beside the plate, tapped it a couple of times with the bat,

and waited for the pitcher to throw. The pitcher wound up once, twice, then raised his left foot and brought his throwing arm around. The next thing Marvin saw was the ball coming at him and the plate.

He swung. Missed!

Jim Cassell was umpire. "Strike!" he said. Then, "Get a little closer to the plate, Marvin. You're too far from it. And keep your feet farther apart."

He tried to do what Jim said. Again he waited for the pitch. He swung! Missed again!

Sweat came on his forehead. He was growing more nervous by the second. If he didn't hit they would see he wasn't any good. And nobody wanted a ballplayer who wasn't good.

The third pitch came in. He watched it closely. He had to hit it now. He was thinking that if he had his own bat, the one Barry had given him, it would have been a cinch. This bat was too heavy.

But it was too late to think of that now.

The ball was here. Straight as an arrow. Chest-high. He swung!

He heard the ball hit into the catcher's glove. The bat carried him almost all the way around.

"Strike three!" said Jim Cassell.

9

BARRY came up the street the next morning wearing a white tee shirt with a large yellow T sewed on the front of it. Marvin wondered what the T stood for.

"Hello, Marv," Barry grinned. "You're just the fellow I want to see."

Marvin's eyes widened. "Me? What do you want to see me for, Barry?"

He wanted to ask Barry about the T, but waited to see what Barry had on his mind.

"We've got a ball game tonight with Attlee Merchants," Barry explained. "If you and your sister and your folks would like to go see it, I can get you tickets."

Marvin's face broke in a big smile. "Gee, Barry! I'd sure like to see the game! Could you wait a minute? I'll run in and ask Mother if we can go!"

Barry smiled. "Sure. Go ahead."

Marvin started to dash away, then remembered. "Barry, what does the T stand for?"

"Taunton," Barry replied.

"Thanks!" Marvin said, then tore away in a run for the big screen door. He darted inside to where his mother was ironing shirts for his father. She looked around at him.

"Well!" she exclaimed. "What are you so excited about?"

"Barry's out there," Marvin said breathlessly. "He said he can get us all tickets to his ball game if we want to go. We can go, can't we, Mother? Please?"

She smiled. "We'll have to wait to see what Daddy says. He won't be home till tonight."

His heart sank. "But he'll go, Mother. I'm sure he will. Daddy loves ball games, too!"

She rested the hot iron on the board and put an arm around him tenderly, pressing him to her. "Yes, he does, honey. I think it will be all right. Go out there and tell Barry we'll go."

"Oh, Mother!" Marvin cried, squeezing her. "You're swell!"

They sat in the grandstand, amid the fans of both teams. The evening was warm, with soft, cottony clouds drifting lazily through the sky, hiding the sun for a minute, showing it again the next. But it was shady and cool in the grandstand. Marvin, Jeannie, and their mother and father were sitting together. Marvin could hardly wait for the game to begin.

Finally the umpire cleared the field of the players who were practicing, announced the batteries, and yelled: "Play ball!"

The Taunton players ran out onto the field. Marvin saw Barry run to first base. He thought he would like to play first base too, on his team. Barry looked nice in his white baseball uniform. *Taunton* was printed on the front of his shirt in blue letters, and on his cap was a T.

Marvin sat straight, on the edge of his seat. This was sure going to be a game to watch!

The first player hit a ground ball to third. The third baseman picked it up

and threw it to Barry. Barry had to stretch way out to snare the ball in order to beat the runner.

"Out!" yelled the umpire, jerking up the thumb of his right hand.

Marvin and Jeannie clapped and yelled with the rest of the Taunton rooters. Finally there were three outs.

Attlee went out to the field and Taunton came to bat.

"Now watch Taunton!" Marvin exclaimed. "Watch Barry get a hit!"

Taunton's first two men grounded out. Marvin's hopes fell. But, he thought, just wait till Barry comes to bat. The third batter walked. When Marvin saw Barry step to the plate swinging two bats, he clapped his hands till they stung. Barry tossed one of the bats back and got in position at the plate.

"Now watch this, Jeannie!" Marvin cried. "Barry will show them how to do it!"

The first pitch was a strike. Barry didn't swing at it. The next was a ball.

Then a strike again. Barry swung and missed.

"Come on, Barry!" Marvin cried loudly. "Hit it! Hit it!"

The pitcher wound up and threw again. Barry swung with all his might. The ball made a loud *plop* in the catcher's glove.

"Strike three!" boomed the umpire. Barry had struck out!

"Oh!" Jeannie sighed.

"Don't worry," Daddy said. "He'll be up again. They can't hit the ball every time."

The innings kept piling up. Finally it was the eighth. The score was tied 1 to 1 and Taunton had one man on second. Barry came to bat. Marvin watched eagerly. So far nobody on either team had done much. It had been a pitchers' battle.

There was the pitch. Barry swung. A hit! Right over the shortstop's head! The runner on second rounded third, ran for home, and scored!

Jeannie and Marvin jumped up and down and yelled till they were hoarse.

The game ended 2 to 1.

"Goes to show," Daddy said in the car as they drove home. "Striking out didn't discourage Barry. You see, he came back and won the ball game, didn't he?"

"You bet!" exclaimed Marvin happily.

10

THE first game in the Grasshoppers League got under way at last. Marvin's team, the Tigers, was playing the Indians. Jim Cassell put Marvin out in left field because Marvin was good at catching fly balls, he said.

The Tigers had first raps. When Jim called off the names of the first three hitters, Marvin was never so surprised in his life as he was to hear his name called off second. He could not understand that, because in every practice he had been hardly able to hit the ball.

Kenny Stokes was first batter. He hit the second pitched ball for a blooping fly to the shortstop. Then Marvin walked to the plate. He wished he had his own bat. He was sure that with his own bat he would hit. It was just perfect for him. He could not find one here that fitted him. As he stood at the plate he felt a shiver go through him. Mother and Daddy were somewhere on the side lines, watching him. He wished they had not come. He didn't want them to see that he could not hit.

The pitcher threw the ball and he

wasn't ready for it. He let it go by. The umpire yelled, "Strike!"

"Come on, Marvin, boy!" He heard Jim's voice from the bench. "Hit it when it's in there!"

He ticked the next one. It went sailing back over the catcher's shoulder, striking the backstop screen.

"You're feeling it!" He heard Jim shout again.

He got ready for the third pitch. With two strikes on him and no balls, he was in a tough spot. His heart thumped against his ribs. He wished Jim had not put him second in the batting order. Everybody would expect too much from him. Down in eighth or ninth, or even seventh position, no-body expected you to hit every time you stepped to the plate.

The pitcher wound up, threw. Marvin put his left foot forward, lifted his bat. But the ball was coming in too wide. He let it go by.

"Ball!" said the umpire.

For a second his heart stood in his throat. Just suppose the umpire had yelled "Strike!"

Now the count was two to one. He felt a little better. The nervousness had partly left him. Again the pitcher wound up, threw the ball. It came in straight and a little low, but it looked as if it might be a strike. He swung.

Missed!

"Strike three!" cried the umpire.

Marvin dropped the bat and walked sadly back to the bench. He did not dare look up. He knew what everybody was thinking.

Jackie Barnes was up next. He hit the ball to the left of second base. Rick Savora followed him and hit the first one for a double. Everybody yelled. The next batter flied out, making it two outs. Then Chuck Sterns hit a grounder through short, scoring Jackie and Rick, and the next batter struck out.

When the Indians came to bat they scored three runs, and went ahead of the Tigers — 3 to 2.

II

IN the third inning, Marvin felt as nervous as he had the first time he had marched up to the plate. Larry Munson, their tall skinny pitcher, was up. He threw right-handed but batted left, something Marvin could not understand. He looked pretty gawky standing with his bat on his shoulder, his legs close together, and the brim of his blue cap bent through the middle like a triangle.

The Indians' pitcher threw a fast one down the center of the plate. Larry let it go, hardly lifting the bat from his shoulder. The next one looked as if it was heading for the same place. This time Larry shifted his right foot and brought his bat around in a hard swing. Crack! His bat met the ball and sent it sailing out to right field!

He ran to first, his long thin legs looking like something in a slow-motion picture, but Marvin could see he was covering ground fast. He circled first base, ran to second and stopped there, standing on the bag with both feet and his hands on his hips. The people roared.

Kenny Stokes, the lead-off man, was up again. He swung at the first ball. It dribbled in a slow grounder toward the pitcher, who fielded it and threw it easily to first.

Larry ran off second base a short distance, then ran back.

Marvin's turn came again. He walked to the plate, his feet feeling like lead weights. He had another bat this time, though he was sure it would not do any good.

"Come on, Marvin!" the boys on the bench yelled. "Bring Larry in! Bring him in!"

His heart was jumping. If he got a hit now probably Larry could make it home to tie the score. Everybody would forget his fanning out in that first inning. He dug his sneakers into the soft dirt — boys in the Grasshoppers League were not supposed to wear cleated shoes — and waited for the pitch.

It came in a little high, but it didn't look bad. Marvin cut at it. He heard a *crack!* as the bat met the ball. A blooper that looked as big as a balloon floated through the air toward the pitcher! Marvin threw down the bat, and started running slowly toward first.

"Run, Marvin!" he heard Jim shout. "Run!"

But the ball dropped into the pitcher's hands. Sadly, Marvin turned and headed back for the bench.

Nobody said anything to him, but he saw Rick suddenly rise from the bench and go toward Jim Cassell. Rick said something to Jim, then Jim turned and spoke to another boy on the bench.

"Artie, play catch with somebody," Marvin heard him say. "You're going in in place of Marvin next inning." He looked up at Marvin. "Marvin — "

"I heard you, Jim," Marvin said. As Rick started back toward his seat on the bench he came face to face with Marvin. Marvin's eyes hardened. His cheeks grew red.

"If you'd give my bat back to me,"
he said angrily, "I could hit that ball!
You're a thief, that's what you are! You
stole my bat!"

12

RICK's face paled and his mouth opened as if he was going to say something. But Marvin was already running out along the left field foul line, his eyes to the ground, not looking right or left. He had to get away from here, just as fast as he could. Someone yelled after him — it sounded like Jim's voice — but he paid no attention to it. He found his glove in the outfield where he had dropped it, picked it up, and kept on running.

He wondered what Jeannie and his mother and father would say. Well — what could they say? They could see that he could not hit the ball. It wasn't any more than right that he was taken out.

He saw a fat, chubby-legged little boy run out into the street chasing after a blue-and-red rubber ball. He wasn't over three years old — a little towhead.

A car whizzed around the corner, its tires screaming on the pavement. Marvin stared at it and then at the little boy. Sudden terror took hold of him. The fat little boy wasn't paying any attention to the car!

Suddenly the loud cry of a woman reached Marvin's ears. "Gary! Gary, get back here! Watch that car!"

There was fear in her voice. Marvin saw her standing in the doorway, one hand clutching her apron, the other on her chest. "Gary!" she screamed again.

The little boy did not move. Realizing that the car would not be able to stop in time, Marvin dove out into the street and picked up the boy, snatching him out of the way.

The car's brakes were squealing. The tires left twin black marks on the street. Then it stopped, and a man looked out of the window, his face ghost-white.

"Boy!" he exclaimed. "That was close!"

"I'll say it was!" said Marvin, with a
shudder. The little boy started to cry
and Marvin carried him to his mother,

who was running toward them from the house. He saw that the back yard of the house faced his back yard.

"Thank you!" she said to Marvin. "Thank you so much!" Marvin saw her white face as she bent and picked up her little son.

A tall, brown-haired man ran out of the house then, followed by a freckle-faced boy who was a year or two younger than Marvin. The boy's shirt was torn, and his corduroy pants had a long rip in one knee. Shakily, the woman told her husband what had happened. The husband looked at Marvin gratefully.

"That was quick thinking, son," he

said. "You sure make us very happy, going after little Gary like that. Sometime I'll see that you get something for this."

Marvin smiled. "That's all right," he said. "I'm glad I came by when I did."

He went home, feeling happy at the man's words.

He had hardly been home five minutes when a soft knock sounded on the door. He knew it wasn't Daddy or Mother. They wouldn't knock.

Wondering, he went to the door and opened it. It was the freckle-faced boy whose little brother he had saved from the path of the car. He was holding a bat in his hand — lifting it up to Marvin.

Marvin's eyes went wide. It was his missing bat!

13

AT the ball field the next afternoon, just before practice, Marvin approached Rick. He had a lump in his throat.

"Rick, I — I'm sorry that I said you had my bat. I got it back yesterday. Freckles Ginty was the one who took it out of my yard."

Rick looked at him a moment before he said anything. Finally he shrugged his shoulders and said, "Okay. You got it back. Maybe you can hit that ball now."

Marvin felt the sarcasm in his voice. He wondered if he and Rick would ever be friends. He wished they would be. Rick was tough in a way, but everybody liked him. He usually wanted his way about things, but he was almost always right, too — and he was a good ball-player. Someday, Marvin thought, Rick might play in the big leagues.

"Did you go in their house?" Rick said suddenly. Marvin had started to turn away, but now that Rick spoke he turned back.

"No," he said. "But Mr. and Mrs. Ginty look like awfully nice people."

"They are. You should see some of

the things Mr. Ginty makes out of wood. Freckles showed me once."

"Nice?"

"Nice? Sometime have Freckles take you in his house. He'll show you!"

"I will!" smiled Marvin.

Thursday afternoon they had another Grasshoppers League game. It was with the Bears. Jim had Artie play instead of Marvin. Artie hit a slow roller the first time up, and was put out. In the field he missed a fly ball that scored a runner for the Bears.

"He can't catch or hit," Kenny Stokes said. "At least, Marv could catch that ball!"

Marvin felt pleased to hear Kenny say that. He was sitting on the bench,

holding the bat in his hand. His own
bat. He had told Jim that he had finally
gotten it back, trying to hint that now
he would be able to hit. But Jim had
only grinned and said that he was glad.

Marvin fidgeted on the bench. He
wished Jim would let him take Artie's
place. He felt sure he could hit now.

Then all at once Jim called to him.
"Okay, Marvin. Go out to left field!"

14

MARVIN dropped his bat under the bench, picked up his glove, and ran out to left field. A fly ball came out to him. He caught it easily.

When it was time to bat he wasn't nervous any more. The bat felt just right in his hand. He felt good. He waited for the pitcher's throw — and the very first pitch he hit for a single!

The crowd yelled. He could hear

Jim's voice — "Thataboy, Marv! I knew you could do it!"

Finally came the sixth inning, the important moment, with the score 8 to 6 in the Bears' favor. The bases were loaded. Marvin again was up to bat. A hit could tie the score. A good long drive could win the ball game. Many a time Marvin had thought of a moment like this, when he would come to the plate with three on. Now it had really happened.

Before he got into the box he rested his bat on the ground, reached down and rubbed some dirt into his palms to dry off the sweat. He had seen Barry do that. Then he picked up the bat and stepped into the box. The pitcher stepped onto the mound, looked at the runner on third, then lifted his arm and threw the ball toward the plate.

It was chest-high. It looked good to Marvin. He put his left foot forward and brought back his bat. He swung, and

the *crack!* sounded throughout the park as bat met ball.

Like a white bullet the ball shot over the shortstop's head. Marvin dropped the bat and scampered for first. The ball hit the grass halfway between the left fielder and the center fielder, who both ran as fast as they could after it. It bounced on beyond them!

One run scored! Two! Three! Marvin ran in from third. One of the fielders picked up the ball and heaved it in. But it was too late.

Marvin crossed the plate — a home run!

It won the game — 10 to 8.

15

THE bat was lucky, all right. Marvin kept on hitting the ball in every game. Jim placed him third in the batting order, just before Rick. At the end of their fifth game his batting average was .453 and Rick's .422. Barry Welton came to see Marvin play whenever he wasn't playing himself. Of course, Jeannie and his mother and daddy never missed a ball game.

Then one day Jim Cassell called Marvin aside. It was after they had won a game that put them in the lead five wins to one loss. Marvin held his bat and glove in his hands as he looked up at Jim. He felt very happy. He had made three hits today, and had walked once. A perfect day at the plate!

Jim said, "Marvin, I've some nice news for you. How would you like to appear on television tonight?"

Marvin's heart jumped. "On television?"

Jim grinned. "Jerry Walker's sports program. He called me up last night. Says he sees by the papers that you're hitting the ball like a major leaguer, and he would like to have you on his program. He would like to ask you a few questions, I suppose."

"Boy! If it's okay with my mother and daddy — I sure would!"

He was bursting with pride when he told the news to them in the car. Their faces brightened with happiness. Jeannie clapped her hands.

"Wait till I tell Annie and Grace!" she cried. "They've got TV sets!"

"Well, you haven't said if I could go," Marvin murmured anxiously.

"Of course you can!" Mother exclaimed, and she pulled out a small handkerchief and wiped her eyes. Daddy smiled big too, but he did not say much. He just gave Marvin a strong hug. Whenever he appreciated something Marvin or Jeannie did, that was what he would always do. Give them a strong hug.

"May I ask Barry to come with us?" Marvin said.

"Certainly," his daddy said then. "You tell Barry and we'll pick him up when we go."

He saw Barry and shouted to him. Barry came over and Marvin told him what his daddy had suggested.

"That would be swell!" smiled Barry.

That night Marvin appeared on Jerry Walker's program. Mother, Daddy, Jeannie and Barry sat in another room, watching through a huge plate-glass window. At first sight of the cameras and lights Marvin was a little frightened and nervous. But by the time the program started, and Jerry Walker talked to him, he felt better. Jerry asked him how long had he played ball? What was his batting average? What did his mother and father think of his playing baseball?

Finally Jerry mentioned his bat. "Jim Cassell tells me you have a bat you won't let anybody else use," he said. "You must think a lot of that bat, Marvin," he added, smiling.

"I sure do," Marvin answered. "It's my lucky bat."

16

WHEN August came, the Tigers and the Bears were tied for first place. The boys were growing more excited by the day. They kept talking about the World Series game. Jim Cassell told them not to let the excitement of it make them forget about playing good baseball. But Marvin and the rest could see that Jim was pretty excited, himself.

"We've three more games to play,"

Jim said. "We must win two out of those three. If we win, we're in!"

They started playing the first of the three games. For the first two innings neither team scored. Then the Bears got on by a bunted ball that caught the Tigers off guard. It must have worried the Tiger pitcher, Larry Munson, because he walked the next man. The third batter hit a single that scored one run. The next batter hit a double to make the score 2 to 0.

A fly went out to left field that Marvin caught easily. The next hitter banged a liner toward Billy Weston at third, who caught it and threw it to second. The runner on second had started to run, thinking it was going for

a hit. He didn't get back in time. The second baseman touched the base and the runner was out.

In the fourth inning the Tigers scored two runs to even it up. It stayed that way till the first half of the sixth. Larry was first batter and got a single, a nice one over first base. Kenny Stokes walked. Then Marvin came up, and everybody cheered.

He swung at the first pitch. Missed! The next one was a ball. The third was in there. He swung hard and hit it — a neat single — but something terrible happened.

The bat broke in two! One piece he had in his hand. The other was flying out across the ground toward third base!

17

MARVIN did not know what to do. Without his bat he was sure everything would be the way it was before. He would not be able to hit again, and Jim would take him out of the game.

There were only two games left to play. The Tigers had won one. They must win one more. If they lost the next two games their chance of seeing a World Series game was gone.

It was a cloudy day. Marvin stayed

inside the house most of the time. He did not feel like going out. He did not feel like doing anything. He wished the baseball season were all over so that there would not be any more ball games. With his bat broken he might

as well quit playing. He would not go out on the ball field now. He knew he could not hit with any other bat. He just knew it.

"It isn't the bat, son," his daddy said to him. "It's you. You've got it in your head that you can't hit with any other bat, and you're wrong."

"But it's true, Daddy!" Marvin cried. "I can't hit with any other bat! I never could! Didn't I try it before?"

His father put a hand on his shoulder, and looked him squarely in the eye. "Look, Marvin," he said softly, "why do you think you can't hit with another bat, and still you were able to hit with the one Barry gave you?"

Marvin shrugged. "I don't know,

Daddy. Maybe there was something about that bat."

His daddy grinned. "Something lucky?"

He shrugged again. "I don't know. Maybe."

"You believe that *bat* was lucky?"

Marvin turned away. He wished his daddy would not talk about it any more. There was no use talking about it.

"I don't know, Daddy. I just know that every time I used that bat I'd hit the ball. I didn't always get a safety, but I'd hit it some place. I never did it with any other bat I used. Never!"

"Just try again," his daddy said. "Just try again, Marvin."

Marvin wished that it would rain on

Friday, the day of their next game.

In the morning it looked as if it was going to rain. But in the afternoon the clouds cleared away and the sun came out bright and hot. Jim still had Marvin bat third. Jim had no idea that a bat made a difference. He was like Daddy.

The first two men up flied out. When Marvin came to the plate he let the first pitch go. It was a strike. He let the next one go. That was a ball. He ticked the third pitch, which made the count one and two. His heart beat faster. From the bench he could hear Jim and Rick yelling:

"Hit it, Marvin! Hit it, boy!"

The fourth pitch came in. He swung — and struck out.

18

MARVIN dropped the bat and ran to the bench after his glove.

"Never mind that, Marv," Jim said. "You'll hit it the next time."

Marvin didn't say anything. When the next time came he would strike out again. Jim would find that out himself. Maybe he didn't believe the bat made a difference, but it did with Marvin. There must have been something about that bat. Striking out his first time up with another bat proved it. How could anybody say it didn't?

He caught a high fly ball that inning. The crowd cheered loudly, but it did not make him feel any happier.

When the Tigers came to bat again he did not have a chance to hit. The Bears' pitcher was too good. He threw hooks that fooled the Tiger hitters. Even Rick struck out.

Marvin trotted back out to the field. That first inning had surely gone fast. The first Bears' hitter stood at the plate and hardly took the bat off his shoulder. Larry was wild with him. Maybe it was because the batter was so small. Larry walked him.

The next batter hit a ground ball that

Kenny missed at short. It rolled to the outfield. Marvin and the center fielder dashed after it. Marvin picked it up and threw it to third. Now there was a man on first and second. Marvin returned to his position in left field and wished no more balls would come out to him.

Crack!

Larry's first pitch was hit for a long fly. It was coming Marvin's way! Marvin got his eye on it and watched it sail into the blue sky. He stepped back a little, then forward, then back again. The ball seemed to be zigzagging. Then suddenly it was curving downward. It was falling fast — dizzily. Marvin put up his gloved hand.

The ball hit the heel of his glove —
and dropped to the ground!

A roar burst from the crowd, died
quickly. Marvin bent, picked up the
ball, and heaved it to the infield. A run-

ner was tearing for home. Another was already on second. The shortstop got the ball and threw it home, but the runner had already scored. The man on second raced to third. The catcher saw him and whipped the ball to third. It sailed over the third baseman's head to the outfield. Marvin went after it. He took his time. He saw that the runner on third was already halfway home.

Three runs! Three runs because he had missed that fly ball! A lump formed in his chest, and grew into a big knot.

The game ended 7 to 4 in the Bears' favor.

19

ONE o'clock Saturday afternoon, and Marvin was still home. The game was scheduled to start at exactly one-thirty. He used to get there at twelve-thirty, or even a few minutes before. Today he did not care. Today he did not want to go at all. He had lost the ball game for the Tigers yesterday by missing that fly ball. He had struck out twice. Sure, he had hit the ball twice, too. But they were grounders, right into somebody's hands. They were not hits.

Not the kind he used to get with his own bat.

That bat was lucky. No matter what Daddy, or Jim, or anybody said. He had never been as good as people said he was. The credit belonged to the bat. Nobody had known that but Marvin. Maybe now they'd find out where the credit had really belonged!

His daddy appeared at the living room door. A frown crossed his forehead, as if he was surprised to see Marvin sitting there.

"Marvin! I thought you had gone to the field?"

Marvin met his eyes, then looked away. His heart started to pound. "I'm not going to the game," he said.

"Why not?"

"Because I'm no good. I can't hit. I can't field. Jim just lets me play because I used to be good."

"That's no way to talk, son," his daddy said, smiling. "Jim lets you play because he knows you're good. You're just thinking about that bat again. And you're wrong. I wish I could make you understand that."

The doorbell chime clanged and his daddy went to answer it. Marvin heard a familiar voice ask for him.

"Marvin!" his daddy called. "Someone to see you!"

Marvin got off the chair. He walked across the room to the door, and stopped. It was Freckles Ginty.

He smiled so that the freckles on his face were almost crawling over each other.

"Hello, Marvin," he smiled. "I got something for you."

Marvin frowned. "What?"

"This!"

From behind his back Freckles pulled a bat. Marvin stared. It was exactly like the one he had broken!

His mouth fell open. For a moment he could not speak. Then he managed to say: "Where — where did you get it?"

"It's the same one you broke," Freckles said, grinning. "My father fixed it together again for you."

20

"STRIKE one!" yelled the umpire. Marvin drew his foot back and rested the bat again on his shoulder. He wasn't worried about having a strike called on him. This was his fourth trip to the plate. Outside of hitting a long fly ball that the center fielder had caught in the third inning, he had two hits. One was a single, the other a triple.

Mr. Ginty had sure paid Marvin back

for saving his little boy on the street that day. Imagine fixing up the bat so that it was like new again! He sure was a wonderful man!

The pitcher threw in another one. "Ball!" said the umpire. "One and one!"

The score was 7 to 5. The Tigers were ahead. There was a man on first. It would not hurt to knock in another run. The Bears were good players. You could not tell when they might start hitting Larry hard and threaten to win the ball game. The team that won this game won the trip to the World Series.

"Come on, Marv!" the gang on the bench shouted. "Come on, kid! Hit that apple!"

Then he heard his daddy. "Come on, Marv! Drive it!"

He felt his heart swell inside him. He seldom heard his daddy shout at the ball games.

Suddenly the pitch came in. He stepped into it and lifted the bat.

He swung. *Crack!* The bat met the ball and it sailed out between left and center fields! He dropped the bat and ran. He touched first, then second, then third — and he did not stop until he crossed home plate!

A home run!

"Hurray! Marv!" everybody roared.

Rick caught him and shook his hand. "Thataboy, Marv! Thataboy!"

"Nice going, Marv!" exclaimed Jim.

"Guess we'll be heading for the World
Series game!"

Marvin grinned. His heart beat so
fast from running and from happiness
he thought it would leap right out of
his shirt.

The Bears lost hope after Marvin's long clout. They didn't score any more runs. The Tigers won — 9 to 5.

Jeannie ran to her brother right after the game and hugged him. Then came his daddy and mother. Then Barry Welton.

"You'll be a big leaguer one of these days, Marvin," Barry smiled.

Marvin returned the smile, then shook his head. "I can't use this bat all my life," he said, holding up the bat. "It'll be too small when I grow up."

Another voice broke in, a soft voice Marvin had heard only once before. "Marvin, I have a confession to make. I hope you'll forgive me if I tell you."

Marvin looked around. It was Mr.

Ginty, Freckles's father. Marvin was puzzled. "What do you mean, Mr. Ginty?" he said.

Mr. Ginty smiled. "I made that bat, Marvin."

Marvin stared. His heart flew to his throat. "You — you mean it isn't the one I used to have? The one that Barry gave me? The one I busted in two?"

"No. It isn't. I don't think I could ever fix that other one up so that you could use it again. This is a brand-new bat. I made it myself — just for you."

Marvin swallowed hard. He put out his hand. Mr. Ginty took it. "Thanks, Mr. Ginty! Thanks — a lot!" Marvin cried.

Then he turned to his daddy. He

could barely see him through the tears
that blurred his eyes. His daddy smiled
back.

"You see? It wasn't the bat, was it,
son?" he said.

Marvin shook his head.

It was himself, all right.

EARTH-SHATTERING FACT FILE

LOCATION: San Francisco, USA

DATE: 18 April 1906

TIME: 5.13 a.m.

LENGTH OF SHOCK: 65 seconds

MAGNITUDE*: 8.3

DEATHS: 700

THE SHOCKING FACTS:

- The quake was the deadliest ever to strike the USA. Two thirds of the city was wiped out. Some 28,000 buildings were destroyed including 80 churches and 30 schools. About 300,000 people were left homeless.

- The city shook because it lay near the San Andreas Fault, a ghastly gash in the Earth's surface. An earthquake deep underground ripped the fault apart.

- San Francisco has grown so much that if such an enormous earthquake struck the city today, it could kill thousands of people and cause billions of dollars of damage.

SAN FRANCISCO

USA

ATLANTIC OCEAN

PACIFIC OCEAN

CALIFORNIA

MEXICO

*That's how seismologists like me measure the size of an earth-shattering earthquake. And this was a seriously big one. You can find out more about measuring earthquakes on page 57.

13

In the nineteenth century, San Francisco had grown from a small village into a brand–new, booming city. No wonder people were proud of their town. And even though many of them lost everything in the earthquake, they knew they could make the city great again. In just a few years, they'd rebuilt the city, bigger and better than ever before. But the danger isn't over yet. Everyone in San Francisco knows only too well that they're living on very shaky ground. Another earthquake could strike anytime. The trouble is no one knows when. But what on Earth makes the seemingly rock–solid ground split apart at the seams? Where does the shocking force come from that can smash a city to smithereens? Forget the nice, tame bits of nature like pretty spring flowers and babbling brooks. This is geography at its wildest. And it's happening right beneath your feet. . . . Are you ready to take the strain?

CRACKING UP

As the shell-shocked people of San Francisco found out, earthquakes are horribly unpredictable. You never know when one's about to strike next. The trouble is shaky quakes usually happen deep underground so it's shockingly hard to spot any warning signs. (Your geography teacher might have eyes in the back of his head but I bet even he can't see through solid rock.) For centuries, earthquakes were so mysterious that people made up stories about them to make sense of what was going on. . .

Shocking earthquake theories
1 The native people of North America thought a giant tortoise held up the Earth. Every time the touchy tortoise stamped its foot, it set off a gigantic earthquake.

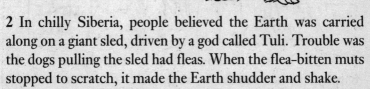

2 In chilly Siberia, people believed the Earth was carried along on a giant sled, driven by a god called Tuli. Trouble was the dogs pulling the sled had fleas. When the flea-bitten muts stopped to scratch, it made the Earth shudder and shake.

I THINK IT'S TIME WE ALL HAD A BATH!

3 Some people in West Africa blamed a love-sick giant. The giant held up one side of the Earth, they believed, while a huge mountain propped up the other and the giant's wife held up the sky. When the soppy giant let his side go to give his wife a hug, guess what? Yep, the Earth shook.

4 In a Central American story, four gods held up the four corners of the Earth. When the Earth got too crowded, they simply shook one corner to tip some people off.

5 People in Mozambique, Africa, thought earthquakes happened when the Earth caught cold. Then you could feel it s-s-s-shaking with a terrible fever. Aaachoo!

6 According to Japanese legend, earthquakes are caused by a giant catfish which lives on the seabed. When the catfish sleeps (you could call this a catnap, ha! ha!), the Earth is nice and still. But when the fish wakes up and starts to wriggle, watch out. That's when you get an earthquake. (It must be a fantastically fidgety fish. Japan's one of the most earthquake-prone places on Earth.)

Could you catch a catfish out? Are you brave enough to save the world? To save the world from an earth-shattering experience, here's what you need to do.

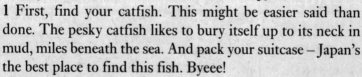

What you need:
- a giant catfish
- a really large rock

What you do:

1 First, find your catfish. This might be easier said than done. The pesky catfish likes to bury itself up to its neck in mud, miles beneath the sea. And pack your suitcase – Japan's the best place to find this fish. Byeee!

2 Find a large (and I mean, *really* large) rock. You might need help with this bit. Do you *know* anyone crazy enough to help you catch a catfish?

3 Put the rock on the catfish's head so it's well and truly pinned to the seabed. Sounds cruel but the shaking should stop. Though you'll be faced with one angry old fish.

Notes:

If you feel weak at the knees just reading this, why not rope in a friendly god to help. The Japanese believed the gods were the only ones with enough power to keep the cranky catfish under control. It was only when the gods went on their holidays that the troublesome shaking began.

A bad case of wind

So, if you believe your legends, earthquakes are caused by a giant fish with a rock stuck on its head. Sounds like a very fishy story. What about any other crackpot theories? Well, there were plenty of those.

The Ancient Greek thinker, Aristotle (384–322 BC), had another earth-shattering idea. He blamed earthquakes on a bad case of . . . wind. Yes, wind. Aristotle thought that earthquakes were caused by great gusts of wind gushing out from caves deep inside the Earth. Apparently, the caves sucked air in, heated it up, then blasted it out again. A bit like a gigantic, deafening fart. (Bet your teacher doesn't tell you this bit.)

But if fusty farts, crabby catfish and soppy giants weren't to blame, what on Earth was making the ground shake? Some religious leaders said earthquakes were God's way of punishing people for their sins. If people mended their wicked ways, the earthquakes would stop. Simple as that. (Whether or not it was true, it was a great way of making people behave better!) One old lady had other ideas. When an earthquake struck London in 1750, she thought it was caused by her servant falling out of bed.

Even horrible geographers got it wrong. In the 1760s, British geographer, John Michell, worked out (correctly) that the Earth shakes because of huge shock waves racing through the rocks. But he also thought (wrongly) that earthquakes were set off by the steam from enormous underground fires.

To tell you the truth, awful earthquakes had geographers stumped. And it might have stayed that way. Luckily, a brilliant German geographer, Alfred Wegener (1880–1930), was determined to get to the bottom of things once and for all. Even if it meant shaking things up a bit. This is his earth-shattering story. . .

Too much on his plate?

As a boy, Alfred Lothar Wegener spent much of his time staring into space. It drove his mother and father mad. They thought young Alfred was wasting his time and would never amount to much. But starry-eyed Alfred proved them wrong. He left school top of the class and went off to university to study astronomy (that's the posh term for learning about outer space). So all that star-gazing turned out to be useful after all. (Why not try this as an excuse next time your teacher catches you staring out of your classroom window?)

NOT DISTURBING YOU WITH MY BORING LESSON, AM I, WATKINS?

NO, SIR. YOU JUST CARRY ON

But even outer space wasn't enough for adventurous Alfred. His other great love was the weather. The stormier, the better. In 1906, he set off for Greenland to study wind. This might not be your cup of tea but Alfred liked it so much he went back again in 1912, 1929, and in 1930. And when he wasn't travelling, he taught meteorology (that's the posh name for studying the weather) and geography at university. Oh yes, Alfred was a real clever clogs.

But even when Alfred was busy teaching, his mind kept wandering to other things. (Does this ever happen to *your* geography teacher?) He really wanted to find out more about how the Earth works. At night, he used to hurry home and scribble his earth-moving ideas down in a notebook. Here's what it might have looked like. . .

My (top) secret notebook by Alfred Wegener

One day in 1910. . .
I'm SO excited, I could burst. It's this cracking idea I've had. It's been worrying away at me for weeks. It all started, you see, when I was showing some of my students where Greenland was on a map. (Call themselves geographers!) Anyway, I suddenly noticed something very strange. Get this. The east coast of South America looked like it fitted snugly into the west coast of Africa. Just like two pieces of a giant jigsaw! But how can that be? Before I get too carried away, I'm going to tear up some newspaper and test out my idea. (I've decided not to tell anyone else about it just yet. Just in case it doesn't work.)

Next day. . .
It works! It works! I tore up the newspaper, like I said. And guess what? The two bits fitted perfectly. It's amazing. You

can hardly see the joins. But there's a very long way to go. I mean, if the two continents were once joined up, how on Earth did they drift so far apart? I really hope I can crack the problem.

Some time later...
I've done it! I really think I've done it this time! And it's ground-breaking stuff, I can tell you. This is what I think has happened. By the way, I've based my ideas on my last Greenland trip when I was watching some icebergs drifting off out to sea. Fascinating things, icebergs. But that's another story. (Sorry the sketches aren't much good.)

1 About 200 million years ago, all the continents (including Africa and South America) were one massive chunk of land. I've called it Pangaea (that's Ancient Greek for "all lands"). I reckon it was surrounded by a huge sea.

2 About 150 million years ago, Pangaea split in two...

3 Then the two big pieces split into lots of smaller bits which began, ever so slowly, to drift apart... Millions and millions

and millions of years later, these bits ended up as the continents we have today (including Africa and South America). Brilliant, eh?

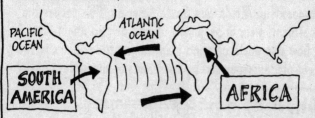

Note: I'm calling my new theory "continental drift". I know it's boring but it'll do for now. Annoyingly, I still can't work out exactly what gets the continents drifting. Never mind. Perhaps it's time to check out some more lovely icebergs.

Two years later...
I've been so busy giving talks about my theory that I haven't had any time for notes. If I'd known it'd be such a shaky ride, I'd have jolly well stuck to teaching. It's been pretty depressing, actually. The problem is no one believes me. No one at all. They say I've made the whole thing up and the whole thing's just coincidence. Pah! See if I care. I'll show them I'm right. If it's the last thing I do. And what's more I can prove it. Ready?

My proof

1 Mesosaurus was an ancient reptile that lived about 300 million years ago. These days it's extinct but get this, you only find its fossils in Africa and South America. This proves that the continents were once joined up and drifted apart later. I mean, how else would you find identical reptile remains in two different places, separated by thousands of kilometres of sea?

OOOH, A POSTCARD FROM MY COUSIN IN AFRICA

2 It's the same with rocks. You get identical rocks in Africa and South America. They're the same age, the same type, in fact, they're a perfect match. And you don't find them anywhere else in the world. So you could say they're rock-solid proof.

TWINS!

3 The weather's another crucial clue. Coal formed millions of years ago. Only in warm, wet places. So Antarctica's out, you might think. Wrong! Coal's been found in icy Antarctica proving the place was once toasty warm . . . and NOWHERE

NEAR the South Pole. You also get the opposite happening. Some of the rocks in Africa and South America are covered in scratches, made years ago by ancient glaciers. So you see, once upon a time, these continents were a lot closer to the South Pole than they are today.

"LET'S GO TO AFRICA" HE SAYS, "NICE AND WARM" HE SAYS...

Hah! And if that doesn't prove I'm right, once and for all, I'm going to Greenland and I'm not coming back! And that's a promise.

MAYBE JUST ONE MORE SWEATER

A very moving story

Sadly, this is exactly what happened. In 1915, Alfred wrote his ideas down in a book, called *The Origin of Continents and Oceans*. Science was pretty stuffy then and the book caused a storm. But still nobody believed a word of it (well, it was *such* a boring title). Many top geologists (they're geographers who study rocks) dismissed his theory as rubbish. One of them called it "Utter, damned rot!" Another said Alfred was "taking liberties with our globe". (To tell the truth, they probably wished they'd thought up the idea themselves.) The main problem for Alfred was that he still couldn't work out what it was that made the continents drift. So he could prove things until he was blue in the face and it counted for nothing. Bitterly disappointed, in 1930 Alfred set off for Greenland. He was never seen again. . .

. . .which means he didn't live to see the day scientists finally believed his theory. For years after Alfred's death, his continental drift idea was completely forgotten. It wasn't until the 1960s that deep-sea scientists made a ground-breaking discovery that proved Alfred right. They found that some bits of the seabed are splitting apart, with red-hot runny rock oozing up through the cracks. When it hits the cold sea water, the hot rock cools, turns hard and builds massive underwater mountains and volcanoes. In other words, the seabed is spreading. But why doesn't the Earth get bigger as the seabed spreads? Where does all the extra rock go? Scientists soon found the answer. In other places, they found, one bit of seabed is being pushed down under the other. Then the rock melts back into the Earth. And guess what? The melting exactly balances out the spreading. This means the Earth always stays the same size. The seabed and the continents are all part of a hard, rocky layer around the Earth, called the Earth's crust. If one bit moves, it shoves the rest along too, as if it's on a colossal conveyor belt. So if the seabed is moving, the continents must be moving too. Alfred had been right all along. The continents are really drifting.

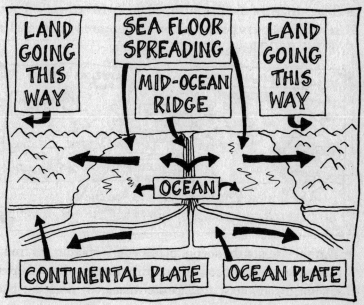

Scientists don't call this "continental drift" any more. They call it "plate tectonics" (teck-ton-iks, from the Ancient Greek word for building). They think this sounds much snappier. Do you?

What on Earth are earthquakes?

OK, you might say, but what on Earth does this have to do with earthquakes? Well, here's what else modern-day geographers have found out:

- The surface of the Earth (called the crust) is cracked into seven huge pieces called plates. (There are lots of smaller pieces, too.) Here's a helpful diagram:

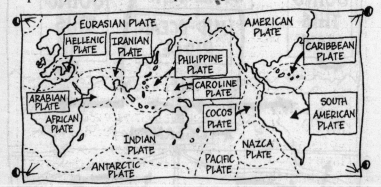

- But they're not the sort of plates you scoff your tea from. These are plates of solid rock which float on top of a layer of hot, bendy rock (called the mantle) – it's a bit like squidgy plasticine.

- Heat from the centre of the Earth (called the core) keeps the rocky plates on the move. (That's the bit that had poor Alfred stumped, remember?) You can't see all these layers from the surface. So here's an interesting X-ray view. . .

CRUST: The Earth's rocky surface. It's the bit you live on.
40 km thick (dry land)
6-10 km thick (seabed)

PLATES: The crust's cracked into pieces. Like a hard-boiled egg you've bashed with a spoon.

MANTLE: The thick, sticky layer below the crust. It's so hot the rocks have melted. The plates float on top of it.
2,900 km
1,980°c

INNER CORE: The centre of the Earth. A solid ball of iron and nickle. It's unbelievably hot but it doesn't melt because of all the other layers pushing down. Heat from the core rises up through the Earth and churns up the Mantle. This churning keeps the crusty plates on their toes.
2,500 km (wide)
4,500°c

OUTER CORE: A boiling hot layer of liquid metal. 2,200 km

CRUST

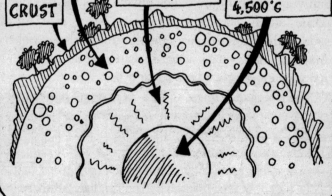

- The earth-shattering plates are always shifting, right beneath your feet. But luckily for you, they move so, so slowly, you usually can't feel a thing. Otherwise, walking to school might get very interesting. Come to think of it, you might never get there at all. . .

- As the plates drift along, they sometimes get in each other's way. It's a bit like being on the dodgems at the fair. As you try to barge your way past another car, you get bashed and scraped, until one of you has to give way. It's a similar thing with plates. They push and shove against each other, and get horribly jammed. (You could try this at home with two bits of sandpaper. Hold them sandy sides together and try to push them past each other with your hands. Any luck?) Over years and years, the pressure builds up and puts the rocks under serious strain. Sometime, something has to give. All of a sudden, the plates jerk apart and the ground shakes violently. And that's how you get an earth-shattering earthquake.

CAN YOU SPOT THE DIFFERENCE ?

① STRESSED-OUT ROCK	② STRESSED-OUT TEACHER
ROCKS UNDER STRESS → ROCKS REACH BREAKING POINT → RUMBLING SOUNDS FROM THE EARTH — CRACKS APPEAR	TEACHER UNDER STRESS → PATIENCE REACHES BREAKING POINT — WRINKLES APPEAR — LOW GROWLING NOISE

Earth-shattering fact
Thank your lucky stars you're not on the moon. Between 1969 and 1977 seismographs (size-mow-grafs)* picked up about 3,000 moonquakes a year. Most of the quakes were caused by meteorites (they're massive great lumps of space rock) smashing into the moon's surface. And if you're wondering how on Earth you find seismographs on the moon, they were left there by moon-walking astronauts.

* Seismographs are posh scientific instruments for measuring earthquakes.

Quick quake quiz

Is your seismic know-how all it's cracked up to be? Is it shockingly good or horribly shaky? Why not try this quick quake quiz to find out. If you've got enough on your plate (ha! ha!), try it out on your geography teacher. It'll have her quaking with fear.

1 How many earth tremors shake the Earth each year?
a) About 100.
b) At least one million.
c) About 10.

2 How long was the longest earthquake?
a) Four minutes.
b) One hour.
c) 30 seconds.

3 Where did the worst ever earthquake strike?
a) Japan.
b) China.
c) Italy.

4 How far away can you feel the shaking?
a) In the next town.
b) In the next country.
c) In the next continent.

5 How often do earthquakes shake Britain?
a) Never.
b) Not very often.
c) More often than you think.

Answers:

1b) Believe it or not, about one million earth tremors shake the Earth every year. That's about ONE EVERY 30 SECONDS. Luckily, most quakes aren't strong enough to rattle a tea cup. Only a few hundred really shake things up. And about 7-11 are truly earth-shattering.

MIND YOUR TEA CUP, DEAR, HERE COMES ANOTHER EARTHQUAKE

2a) The awesome earthquake which struck Alaska in March 1964 lasted for four earth-shattering minutes. That's about the time it takes for you to get in from school, grab a can of pop, turn on the telly and veg out in your favourite armchair. No time at all really. But for the people who lived through this terrible ordeal, it must have felt like a lifetime. It was one of the strongest earthquakes known. Most earthquakes last for less than a minute. By the time you'd opened your pop, the shaking would be over. But in earthquake terms, even less than a minute is plenty long enough.

WHEN'S THIS EARTHQUAKE GOING TO STOP?

3b) Unfortunately, earthquakes are often rated by numbers of lives lost. And big quakes can be big killers. Experts estimate that 830,000 people died in the quake that struck Shaanxi, China, in January 1556. Making it the deadliest quake in history. Many people lived in caves carved out of the cliffs which crumbled apart around them. The deadliest quake of recent times was the one that struck Tangshan, China, in July 1976. It reduced the city to rubble. As many as 500,000 people lost their lives. A million more were injured.

4c) The colossal quake that hit Lisbon, Portugal, on 1 November 1755 was the worst European earthquake ever. The shaking was felt as far away as Hamburg and even the Cape Verde Islands – a massive 2,500 km away. It lasted for 6-7 minutes, which in earthquake time is a very long shake up!

5c) You're most likely to experience an earthquake if you live in California or Japan (check out the next chapter to find out why). But even Britain isn't totally tremor-free. Unbelievably, Britain has up to 300 or more earthquakes a year. Luckily, most are far too faint to feel. But not all of them. In April 1884, the people of Colchester in Essex got a nasty shock when a medium-sized earthquake shook the town, toppling several church spires and destroying 400 houses. In the villages near by, hundreds of chimney stacks tumbled down but nobody was killed. When a quake hit Shropshire in 1996 no one was hurt, but a hamster tumbled out of its cage. Poor thing!

IT'S A SHOCKING LIFE BEING A HAMSTER

Horrible Health Warning...

Earthquakes can seriously damage your health. Even though the Earth shook for less than an hour all together in the twentieth century, killer quakes caused more than two million deaths. DON'T PANIC. You're much more likely to be struck down by the flu. Still worried? Instead of sitting there shaking like a leaf, why not hurry along to the next earth-shattering chapter? It'll tell you where earthquakes are likely to happen so you know which places to avoid...

WHOSE FAULT IS IT?

Some places are deadlier than others. Take your geography classroom, for example. Think of all the horrors lurking behind that door. Geography books, geography tests, and worse still, geography teachers. Horrible. Now think of being on holiday. You're relaxing on a sandy beach after a dip in the warm, blue sea. (Where would *you* rather be?) It's the same with the stressed-out old Earth. Some places are barely bothered by earthquakes. Any tremors simply pass them by. Other places are on seriously shaky ground. A killer quake may be only seconds away. So where on Earth are these quake-prone zones?

Quick quake guide

Remember how the Earth's rocky crust is cracked into pieces called plates? Well, you'll find most of the shakiest places on Earth where two pushy plates meet up. In fact, this is how 95 per cent of all earthquakes happen. The exact type of earthquake you get depends on exactly how the plates behave. Feeling under pressure? Don't worry. Here's seismic Sid with his quick quake guide.

Hi, Sid here. Sizing up earthquakes is simple really. Once you know what you've got on your plate. Get two rock-hard plates together and something's got to give. . .

1 Pulling apart

In some places, you get two plates pulling apart. Red-hot, runny rock from the Earth's mantle oozes up to plug the gap. All that pulling sets off lots of small-ish earthquakes. Or you could call them seaquakes (well, they take place in the sea bed). Most of these quakes happen underwater, far from any land. So they're pretty harmless, unless, of course, you happen to be a fish. . .

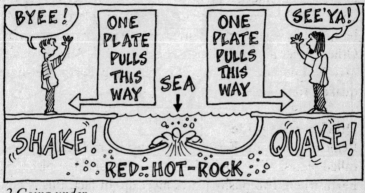

2 Going under

In some places, you get two plates crashing head-on in a colossal collision. One plate gets pushed under the other plate and its rocks melt back into the Earth. If you're planning a holiday near the coast, watch out. Slowly but surely, the seabed might be sinking under the land. Triggering off some of the worst earthquakes of all.

3 Slipping and sliding

In some places, you get two pushy plates trying to shove past each other. If they slide by nice and gently you get lots of tiny tremors. They're nothing to worry about and don't do much harm. But if one plate gives suddenly, beware. You could be in for a truly earth-shattering shock.

Earth-shattering fact
If you like living dangerously, why not hop in a boat and head off for the Pacific Ocean. It's lovely and warm and blue. But be careful. Deadly danger lurks in its depths. The land around the edges of the Pacific is the shakiest on Earth. This is where huge segments of seabed are sinking under the land, setting off massive earthquakes. In fact, three-quarters of all earthquakes happen here. Still going?

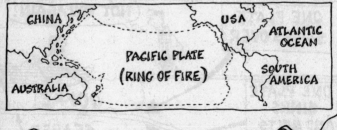

Teacher teaser

If you want to give your teacher a shock, put your hand up politely and ask him or her this harmless-sounding question:

PLEASE, SIR, WHY DID THE MISSISSIPPI RIVER RUN BACKWARDS?

ER... MISS, WHO?

Is this a trick question?

Answer: No, it isn't. In the winter of 1811–1812, the state of Missouri, USA, was struck by three of the worst earthquakes in American history. Each quake made the Earth shake more than 1,600 km away. And if that wasn't shocking enough, the quake caused the Mississippi River to change course completely and start to flow north instead of south. No wonder the fish were worried.

The fish weren't the only ones who got a nasty shock. The quake took everyone by surprise. You see, Missouri was the last place on Earth you'd expect to get an earthquake. It's nowhere near the edge of a plate. Seismologists now reckon that about five per cent of earthquakes happen in the middle of plates, probably along cracks left by ancient earthquakes. Trouble is, they don't know where these cracks are.

39

Finding fault

While your geography teacher's having her teabreak, knock on the staffroom door. Make up an excuse like, "Please, Miss, I want to be a seismologist when I leave school. Do I have to be good at geography?" While she's replying, sneak a good look at the mug she's using for her tea. Is it horribly chipped and cracked? Would one good tap shatter it into pieces? (Only try this if you *want* to do extra homework for the rest of your school days.)

Funnily enough, the stressed-out Earth is a bit like your teacher's old mug. How? Well, its surface is criss-crossed by millions of cracks.

The deepest cracks mark where two plates meet. Of course, horrible geographers don't call them cracks. They've thought up something much more boring. The tricky technical name is faults. But they're not the sort of faults your mum or dad mean when they tell you off for being untidy or picking your nose. These faults are weak spots in the Earth's crust, like the cracks in your teacher's mug. Pile on the pressure and these faulty rocks snap, triggering off earth-shattering earthquakes.

Geographers pick out three types of fault, depending on how the rocks move. Here are Sid's top tips for telling these fickle faults apart.

SID'S SEISMIC NOTE BOOK...

1 Normal fault. Watch out for places where two crusty plates are pulling apart. Tell-tale signs are where you see one slippery plate sliding under another.

FAULT LINE

PULLS

PULLS

SLIDING UNDER

RATHER NICE PICNIC AREA

2 Reverse fault. This time you get two plates being pushed together. A dead giveaway is when one plate starts sliding up over the other.

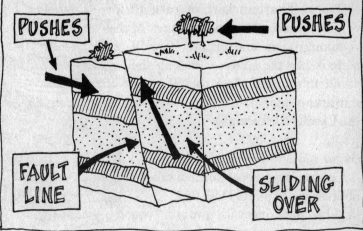

PUSHES

PUSHES

FAULT LINE

SLIDING OVER

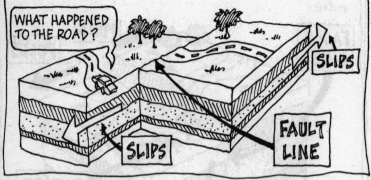

3 Strike–slip fault. This is where two plates are sliding past each other. One slips one way. The other slips the other way. Very slippery characters. This means that fences or roads that once matched up don't match up any more.

WHAT HAPPENED TO THE ROAD?

SLIPS

SLIPS

FAULT LINE

Are you brave enough to pick fault in a fault?
To find out more about how strike-slip faults tick, why not try this tasty experiment. Go on, it's a piece of cake.

What you need:
- A cake (for the Earth's crust). *Note*: The best sort of cake to use is one with lots of layers of sponge, jam and cream. They'll look like the layers of rock in the Earth's crust. And they'll taste yummy, too.
- A knife. (Be careful.)

What you do:
1 Cut two large, gooey slices of cake.
2 Press the two slices together.
3 Now pull one slice towards you

and push the other away from you so they squidge by sideways. Congratulations! You've just demonstrated how a strike-slip fault works (well, almost). Simple, eh?

4 Now eat the bits of cake. Delicious!

P.S. Sick note: You can adapt this activity for the other two types of faults, too. But don't blame me if eating all that cake makes you feel horribly sick. If you do, that's your fault.

Faults – the shocking facts

1 The most famous fault on Earth snakes across sunny California, USA. Here the Earth's literally splitting apart at the seams. This crazy crack's called the San Andreas Fault and at any time now it could shake California to the core.

2 From the air, the fault looks like a ghastly scar running across the landscape. It's about 15–20 million years old and about 1,050 kilometres long, with lots of smaller faults running off it. No wonder California's feeling the strain. It suffers more than 20,000 tremors a year.

3 The fickle San Andreas Fault marks the place where the North American Plate (on the east) meets the Pacific Plate (on the west). It's a strike–slip fault (remember those?) which means the plates are sliding past each other. Actually, both plates are sliding in the same direction. But because the Pacific Plate moves much faster than the North American, it looks like they're pulling in opposite ways.

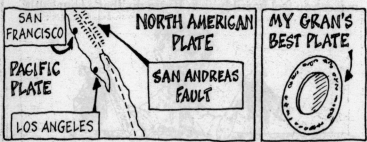

4 For most of the time, the plates slip by smoothly and trigger only tiny tremors. Creepy geographers call this creeping along. Sometimes, though, the plates get horribly jammed. The pressure builds up . . . and up . . . and up, until one plate gives way under the strain and the other plate jerks forwards.
5 You might think any sensible person would prefer to keep their feet on much firmer ground. But you'd be wrong. Horribly wrong. If mingling with famous film stars is your cup of tea, head for Los Angeles (the home of Hollywood). About 14.5 million people live in the city, perilously close to the San Andreas Fault. Another big city, San Francisco, sits practically on top of it. And, as you know, San Francisco's horribly earthquake prone. Remember the disastrous 1906 quake?
6 Seismologists say the most fragile bits of the fault are the north and south ends. They've been storing up trouble for centuries. And they could reach breaking point at any time . . . with catastrophic consequences. As they've done

many times before. Time to pay a second visit to shaky San Francisco. . .

The Daily Globe

18 October 1989, San Francisco, California, USA

CITY REELING FROM KILLER SHOCK

The stunned residents of San Francisco are still reeling from the shock today after yesterday's massive earthquake. Measuring 7.1 on the Richter Scale, it was the biggest quake to hit the city since the Great Quake of 1906. Once again, San Francisco has been shocked to the core.

The quake struck the city in the early evening, at the height of the rush hour. Thousands of people had already left work and were on their way home. The freeways were jammed with rush hour traffic. Pedestrians packed the pavements, chatting or stopping for a beer. At the Candlestick Football Park, the game was already in full flow. The San Francisco

Giants were playing Oakland in the American Baseball World Series. Some 62,000 fans had packed the stadium to cheer their team on. All in all, just a normal day in the life of our busy city.

Then, at 5.04 p.m., disaster struck. In the Santa Cruz mountains to the south of the city, a section of the San Andreas Fault snapped suddenly under centuries of strain.

SNAP TO IT

A 40-kilometre crack ripped the Earth open. Just six short seconds later, the shock waves reached San Francisco. . .

For 15 seconds, the city was shaken to its core.

Fifteen seconds that seemed like for ever.

SHAKY START

Reports just reaching us put the death toll at about 68 but with thousands more people injured or missing. All over the city, buildings have been toppled and smashed apart. A 1.5-kilometre stretch of the freeway has snapped in two and collapsed, crushing motorists underneath. Elsewhere in the city, thousands of homes and businesses lie in ruins.

The worst-hit parts of the city are those around the bay, which were built on land reclaimed from the sea. Here houses and apartment blocks have simply sunk into the soft ground.

With the risk of aftershocks a real possibility, the city's emergency services have lost no time clearing the streets. Their advice to everyone is to go home, turn off the gas (in case of fire) and stock up on food and bottled water.

HEAD HOME

Now the terrible task of rescuing the injured from the rubble can begin in earnest.

The clean-up of the city will take many years. Rebuilding people's shattered lives will take even longer. But most San Franciscans realize they have been lucky this time. They know it could have been worse. Much worse.

For some time now, seismologists have been predicting the Big One. No one knows if this was it. An even more powerful quake may be just round the corner. Despite everything, it's a risk many people are willing to take. Asked if she would now leave the city, one woman told us,

"Why should I? This is my home. Anyway, I survived the last one, didn't I? What are the chances of being in another?"

HOME SWEET HOME

Only time will tell. . .

EARTH-SHATTERING FACT FILE

LOCATION: San Francisco, USA
DATE: 17 October 1989
TIME: 5.04 p.m.
LENGTH OF SHOCK: 15 seconds
MAGNITUDE: 7.1
DEATHS: 68
THE SHOCKING FACTS:

• The city's major skyscrapers swayed by several metres but did not fall down. Still, the quake was horribly costly, causing almost $6 million (£4 million) of damage.

• In the year after the earthquake, more than 7,000 aftershocks were recorded around San Francisco. Five of them measured more than 5.0 on the Richter Scale.

• For such a big earthquake, the death toll was low. Thanks to the brilliant emergency services (fire, police and ambulance). In cities like San Francisco, the emergency services are trained to be ready and waiting when a quake strikes. An alarm sounds to give them a 20-second warning. It doesn't sound long but it's long enough to get rescuers and equipment in place, fast.

SAN FRANCISCO · USA · ATLANTIC OCEAN · PACIFIC OCEAN · CARIBBEAN SEA · SOUTH AMERICA

While you're still in shock, here's a warning about the next chapter. This book has got off to a very shaky start. But things are about to get worse. Feeling brave? You'll need to be as you wave goodbye to this earth-shattering chapter and crash into the next one. . .

LEAD ON!

Shattering Shock Waves

Picture another scene. This time you're not at home in bed. You're sitting in your classroom, snatching another quick snooze. Suddenly, the Earth starts to shake. You wake up with a start. The windows are rattling, your teeth are chattering, books and pencils are flying everywhere. . . What on Earth is going on? DON'T WORRY. It might feel like you've been struck by an earthquake but thankfully you haven't. It's only your geography teacher exploding with rage.

BOOM! WHAAAGGH!

A real–life earthquake's a million times more mind-blowing. (If you can imagine that.) And, believe it or not, all this mayhem and chaos is down to a bunch of waves. . .

What on Earth are shock waves?
Forget the waves you see rippling across the sea. The sort that give you a soaking when you're swimming or capsize your canoe. These waves aren't wet or windswept. No wonder you're confused. Time to call in Sid, our expert. . .

WHAT ON EARTH ARE THESE WAVES, THEN, IF THEY'RE NOT WET?

They're gigantic waves of energy. Don't worry, I'll explain. For years and years, strain builds up in the rocks until, one day, they go snap. Like a gigantic Christmas cracker. Then where does all that pent-up energy go? It blasts out through the surrounding rocks in gigantic, wobbly waves, that's where. You can't see this sort of wave. In fact, you can't feel them . . . until they hit the surface and give the Earth a really good shake.

WEIRD. WHAT ELSE SHOULD WE KNOW ABOUT THESE SHAKY WAVES?

Well, for a start, there are several different sorts. When they were discovered, geographers got horribly excited and gave the waves boring names. Pretty sad, eh? Want to know what the waves are called? Sure about that? OK, here goes. . .

1 Body waves. These waves travel through the Earth's insides until they reach the surface. There are two main types:

- *P waves.* These waves make the rocks squash and stretch, like a massive spring. You press the spring down, then ping! It springs back again. It's the same with the rocks. The P stands for primary because these pushy waves reach the surface first. Well, I warned you the names were boring.

- *S waves.* These waves race through the rocks in ripples, like when you hold the end of a rope and give it a good shake. The S stands for secondary because, guess what, they're the second to surface.

2 Surface waves. These waves shoot through the Earth's surface, shaking the ground up and down.

In the past, it was all the rage to name waves after horrible geographers. Now I know this doesn't sound very cool to you but the poor things considered it a great honour. Two of the most famous (waves and geographers) were called Love and Rayleigh.

- *Love waves.* After ace British geographer A. E. Love (1863–1940). He came across them while he was a professor of science at Oxford University. Love waves shift rocks from side to side.

- *Rayleigh waves.* After posh John Strutt, Lord Rayleigh (1842–1919). Lord Rayleigh was filthy rich and had his own private laboratory in his posh mansion. He was also a professor of physics at Cambridge University. Even though he'd been a sickly child, John was sickeningly brainy. He didn't have to go to school (how lucky can you get?). His rich dad hired a private tutor so he could do his lessons at home instead. John loved science and maths (strange but true) and he also liked travelling. In fact, he had lots of his best ideas on holiday. Amongst other things, he worked out why the sky is blue and discovered a new gas in the atmosphere. For this, he won the Nobel Prize for Physics in 1904. He also discovered a type of surface wave which moves through rocks in a rolling action.

ROCK 'N' ROLLIN' PROFESSOR

ROLLIN' ROCKS

HMM. BUT HOW DID THEY KNOW WHERE THE WAVES WERE, IF THEY COULDN'T SEE THEM?

Good point. You're smarter than you look. Actually, it was a mixture of using their imaginations and being brilliant at maths. First, they tried to imagine what the insides of the Earth looked like. Then they used maths to work out where the waves would be. Sounds like horribly hard work? Lucky I've brought a picture along. . .

AN EARTHQUAKE: the inside story

FOCUS: The spot underground where the rocks first go snap. It's also called the hypocentre. This is where the waves start from. It can be very deep down (over 300km); medium deep (300-70km) or shallow (less than 70km).

EARTH'S CRUST

EPICENTRE: The bit of the Earth's surface directly above the earthquake's focus. The bit that usually shakes the most.

ELASTIC SHOCK WAVES: Blast upwards and outwards from the focus.

EARTH'S MANTLE

EARTH'S CORE

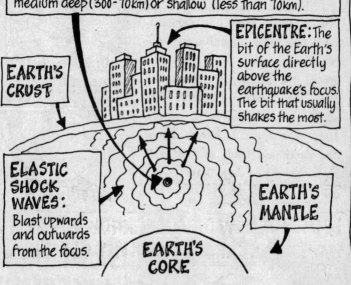

ARE THE DEEPEST EARTHQUAKES THE WORST?

Not necessarily. Deep quakes are stronger, it's true. But shallow quakes do more damage. Usually. This is because the waves don't have far to travel from the focus to the surface. So they don't lose power. They shake the ground horribly strongly but only a small bit of it. Deep quakes feel less shaky but cover more ground.

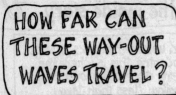

HOW FAR CAN THESE WAY-OUT WAVES TRAVEL?

The waves from a seriously earth-shattering earthquake can travel thousands of kilometres around the Earth. Take the quake that hit Chile in 1960. The surface waves were so strong they whizzed 20 times around the Earth and could still be felt more than two days later.

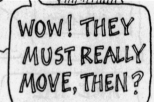

WOW! THEY MUST REALLY MOVE, THEN?

Sure do. P waves (remember them?) are the fastest. They speed along at an awesomely quick six kilometres a second in the crust. That's like travelling from London to Paris in a minute! Ear-witnesses have reported hearing a loud roar as the waves hit the surface. S waves aren't far behind, followed by slower, surface waves. But the different types of rocks they race through can make the whizzy waves speed up or slow down.

Now you're a whizz with waves, you can put them to good use. Unlike Love and Rayleigh, seismologists don't have to guess what the Earth's insides look like anymore. They use shock waves to suss out about the rocks. They also use shock waves to work out just how horribly violent an earthquake is. Read on to find out more.

Scales of destruction

So how do you measure exactly how earth-shattering an earthquake is? It's shockingly difficult even for the experts. Why? Well, where on Earth do you start? With the earthquake's power? The damage it does? Or the size of the crack that caused it? In fact, geographers measure all three things. Which makes life horribly confusing. Here's Sid again to try to make sense of three of the handiest earthquake scales. Which one do you think works best?

A

Name: The Modified Mercalli Scale

What it measures: Earthquake intensity. This means how strongly the earthquake shakes the Earth and the damage it does. Records of earthquake intensity are great for studying ancient earthquakes. More importantly, they allow emergency services to be ready when an earthquake strikes. It's like listening to a rock band playing REALLY LOUD music. . . And they don't come much louder than the one, the only, the truly earth-shattering QUAAAKKES!

You can think of intensity as how loud the band sounds to your ears alone, no matter where you're standing in the concert hall – front, middle, back or even outside it.

THE DAMAGING DETAILS:

EARTHQUAKES ARE RATED ON A SCALE OF I (1) TO XII (12). HERE'S HOW THE SCALE WORKS...

I	Too weak for people to feel.	
II	Felt by a few people, upstairs in buildings.	
III	Felt indoors. Feels like a lorry rumbling past.	
IV	Felt outdoors. Rattles windows, rocks parked cars.	
V	Shakes buildings. Cracks plaster on walls.	
VI	Felt by everyone. Moves furniture. Shakes trees.	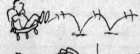
VII	Damages buildings. Loose bricks fall. Hard to stand up.	
VIII	Major damage to buildings. Breaks tree branches.	
IX	Cracks appear in ground. Buildings collapse.	
X	Buildings destroyed. Landslides. Water slops out of rivers.	
XI	Few buildings left standing. Railway lines bent.	
XII	Near total destruction.	

What the experts say:

This scale's a bit hit and miss, I'm afraid. Trouble is it relies on what people see and feel. Ask five different people and they'll say five different things. So, you'd have five different grades for the same earthquake. See what I mean? And the intensity changes depending on where you're standing. (So when the Quakes played "Shake, rattle 'n' roll", it sounded really loud to you because you were standing right at the front. But your mate who turned up late and was stuck outside heard a quieter version.) Besides, who wants to hang around and check out the damage?

Earth-shattering fact
You can use anything to measure intensity. Even a horse. In Australia, some people compare the shaking felt in a slight earthquake to a horse scratching its back on a fence.

B
Name: The Richter Scale
What it measures: Earthquake magnitude. This means how much energy an earthquake releases when the rocks break. (It's this energy that shoots along in seismic waves.) Remember the Quakes? Sorry, REMEMBER THE QUAKES? Imagine listening to a solo on Johnny Shake's lead guitar. Making allowances

for how close you're standing to the stage. So that it sounds just as LOUD wherever you are.

The damaging details:

The Richter Scale was named after top American seismologist Charles F. Richter (1900–1985). In 1935 Charles was put in charge of the Seismological Laboratory in a company called Caltech, in quake-prone California, USA. It was a plum job for a young man. But Charles wasn't bothered about fame and fortune. No. He was utterly fed up. Fed up with answering the phone all day to boring old journalists, asking the same boring old question,

You see, at that time, the only way of sizing up earthquakes was with the Modified Mercalli Scale. Trouble was, you never got the same answer twice. It was hopelessly unreliable. Grumpy Charles Richter scratched his head. He had to find something better. Something that even those pesky journalists could understand. Then Charles had a brainwave. He compared the time it took for the different waves to show up on his seismograph, to figure out how far away the earthquake was. Then he measured how far and how fast the ground was shaken about by the shock waves at the place where his seismograph was. Then, making allowances for how far away and how deep the earthquake was, he calculated how powerful it was. (Phew! It's complicated.) It was much more accurate and scientific. Charles's new, improved scale looked something like this:

0 - The tiniest tremors recorded

1 - Only felt by instruments

2 - Barely felt even near epicentre

3 - Felt near epicentre but little damage

4-5 - Felt further away. More damage

6 - Fairly destructive

7 - Major earthquake

8 - Great earthquake

hamster damage

And it doesn't stop there. Modern, ultra-sensitive seismographs can record really teeny tremors, down to –2 or –3. But don't think a magnitude 7 earthquake is only a little bit worse than a magnitude 6. On the Richter scale, each step up means a 10-fold increase. So a 7 is actually 10 times bigger than a 6 but only a tenth as big as an 8. Got it?

What the experts say:

This scale's always a popular choice. It's the one they use on the telly. The only snag is it can't really cope with megaquakes. (They're the ones above 8.5.)

C
Name: The Moment Magnitude Scale
What it measures: Seismic moment. This measures the total size of an earthquake. The whole shocking lot. Meanwhile, back at the Quakes concert. . . Make allowances for how far you're standing from the stage. Then take out your earplugs and it's still like listening to the whole ear-splitting band, turned up really LOUD!

The damaging details:
This scale takes everything into account, from the first crack in the rocks, to how much the Earth shakes and how long the earthquake lasts.

What the experts say:

This scale is the experts' choice. It's tricky to calculate but awesomely accurate because it gives the whole earth-shattering picture. And it's brilliant for those really big quakes, between 9 and 10. So brilliant, in fact, that some of the biggest quakes have been upgraded. The 1960 Chile megaquake measured 8.5 on the Richter scale. Pretty big, you'd think. True, but actually it was much, much bigger than that. Its moment magnitude is now rated as 9.5, making it one of the most massive quakes ever.

Killer quakes
The catastrophic Chile quake was the most powerful quake of the twentieth century. But in the worst earthquakes ever, it doesn't even make the top ten. That's because many earthquake lists are based on the numbers of people killed. It's tragic but true. In Chile's case, some 2,000 people lost their lives. Which was pretty bad. But for such a great quake, it was amazing there were so many survivors.

TOP TEN EARTHQUAKES

LOCATION	DATE	DEATHS	MAGNITUDE
10: Chihli, China	1290	100,000	Unknown
9: Kanto, Japan	1923	142,000	8·3
8: Ardabil, Iran	893	150,000	Unknown
7: Nan-Shan, China	1927	200,000	8·3
6: Gansu, China	1920	200,000	8·2
5: Damghan, Iran	856	200,000	Unknown
4: Aleppo, Syria	1138	230,000	Unknown
3: Tangshan, China	1976	242,000	7·9
2: Calcutta, India	1737	300,000	Unknown
1: Shaanxi, China	1556	830,000	8·3

NB: Some of these earthquakes were so long ago that experts have had to estimate their magnitude. But if they were big enough to go down in history, they must have been pretty bad!

Some of these quakes happened a long time ago when there weren't any accurate records. So the numbers of deaths are based on guesswork. The true numbers might be much higher . . . or much lower. There's really no way of telling.

One thing's for certain. Earth-shattering earthquakes are horribly dangerous. And they can happen almost anywhere, at any time. So to be on the safe (well, safe-ish) side, surely it's best to stay away from places known to be prone to quakes? You'd think so, wouldn't you? You really would. But plenty of people would disagree. . .

"ON "VERY" "SHAKY" GROUND"

What do places like San Francisco, Los Angeles, Mexico City and Tokyo have in common? Give up? The answer is they're some of the biggest and busiest cities on Earth. And they're all built on very shaky ground. So why on Earth do people live in such horribly hazardous places? After all, a big quake could raze a big city to the ground in a matter of seconds. Amazingly, some 600 million people still live in quake-prone zones. Despite the appalling dangers. If you ask them why they don't just move out and go and live somewhere safer, they'll probably reply that for most of the time they're as safe as houses at home.

Besides, the worst may never happen. But then again, it just might. . .

Catastrophe in Kobe

Kobe is a bustling city in southern Japan. It's one of Japan's biggest ports and an important centre of industry. Unfortunately, earthquakes shake Japan regularly, though there hadn't been a big quake in Kobe for some time. Until 17 January 1995, that is. So what does it feel like when your world's shaken apart? Here's how the events of that fateful day might have appeared to a young boy.

the earthquake by yoshi

We learned all about earthquakes at school. So I knew Japan got loads of them. Sometimes we did earthquake drills. But they were pretty boring. Anyway I wasn't a bit worried. Kobe's a really brilliant place. I've lived here all my life. It's really nice and safe. Besides, I didn't really believe in earthquakes, anyway. But I do now...

Last Tuesday, things got really scary. It was early in the morning and I was fast asleep. Next thing I knew, I was thrown out of bed on to the floor. The floor was shaking. But that wasn't all. We live in a block of flats and it wasn't just the floor shaking. The whole building was shaking. It was really scary. It was dark and I didn't know what to do. I could see things skidding across the floor. I guessed it must be my bookcase and my bed. To make matters worse, there was a terrible noise, like a monster roaring. I heard my mum calling to me and my sister. Then my dad came into my bedroom with a torch. He told me to go into the kitchen and get under the kitchen table, like we'd been taught at school. I wish I'd taken more notice. It was hard to stand up and walk but I did what my dad said and went to the kitchen. My sister was crying and hugging my mum. You see, she's only five. I was scared too but I tried not to show it. The shaking seemed to last for ever

and ever. Then, at last, it stopped. Mum and Dad held our hands tightly and we ran out of the flats into the street. Outside, things were really bad. It was just getting light so we could see all the damage. Our building wasn't too badly hit but the block next door had toppled over and smashed to smithereens. It was the same all the way down our street. Half the houses had collapsed. It took a bit of getting used to. You think people's houses will last for ever. Some of them were my friends' houses. I really hoped they were safe. And there were these huge cracks in the pavement. Everything was ruined. One man said it was like a giant had stamped on the city and squashed it flat.

I sat on the pavement with my mum and my sister while my dad went to see if he could help. There were lots of people just sitting there, staring. My mum said it must be the shock. Anyway, I wasn't even frightened anymore. I was just sad and I was really cold. We left our house in such a rush we didn't bring our coats or anything with us. At least my mum and dad and sister are safe. Our next-door neighbour was trapped in the rubble and my dad helped pull her out. I was really proud of him. But there were lots of people shouting and crying because they couldn't find their friends and relatives. It was really horrible.

I don't know how long we waited in the street. It felt like hours. Then later that day, my dad fetched us and took us to a hall in another part of the city which wasn't so badly damaged. The hall belongs to the steel company my dad works for. Dad says his company will look after us for the time being. We can't go home because there's no water or gas or electricity, and our house isn't safe. The hall's really noisy and crowded because there are lots of other families here.

But a man came and gave us some warm blankets and food. It was only rice-balls to eat but I was so hungry I didn't care. And it stopped my sister crying. Mum said that other people were staying in schools or shrines. And that all of us were the lucky ones. I'm glad we didn't have to stay in my school.

It's OK here and I've made some new friends but I don't know how long we'll be staying. Still, Dad says I must put a brave face on it and look after my little sister. I told him I'll try. But it isn't easy. Especially as Dad thinks we might be in for some aftershocks. They're little shocks after the big earthquake. I really, really hope he's wrong. I don't want to have anything to do with an earthquake ever again. I just want to go home.

EARTH-SHATTERING FACT FILE

DATE: 17 January 1995
LOCATION: Kobe, Japan
TIME: 5.46 a.m.
LENGTH OF SHOCK: 20 seconds
MAGNITUDE: 7.2
DEATHS: 4,500; 15,000 injured
THE SHOCKING FACTS:

• It was the deadliest quake to hit Japan since the Great Kanto Earthquake of 1923 when 142,000 people died.

• The quake caused massive destruction. Some 190,000 buildings were damaged even though many were meant to be earthquake-proof. Fire burned thousands more buildings down.

• The Hanshin Expressway, the raised main road linking Kobe to Osaka, keeled over on its side. Because it was early morning, the road was almost deserted. A few hours later and it would have been packed with cars.

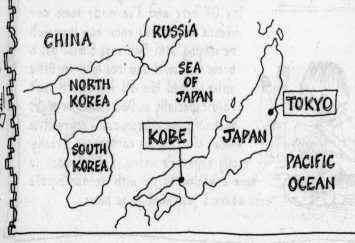

70

Seismic side effects

Smashing up cities seems shocking enough. But earthquakes have plenty of other nasty surprises in store. Here are some seismic side-effects you might want to steer clear of:

1 Earthquake ups and downs. Earth-shattering earthquakes can change the face of the landscape. So you might have trouble working out where you are. Some land sinks. Some's shoved up several metres into the air. Roads and railway lines that once met in the middle, don't meet anymore. In the 1964 Alaska earthquake, a chunk of land THE SIZE OF FRANCE tilted to one side. It left the fishing village of Cordova so far from the sea that the tide no longer reached the harbour! Leaving the fishermen's boats high and dry. Other normally dry places were flooded.

71

2 Lethal landslides.
On 31 May 1970, an earthquake measuring 7.8 on the Richter scale shook Peru. But worse was to come. The earthquake triggered off a lethal landslide on Mount Huascaran. It sent millions of tonnes of rock and ice hurtling downhill at devastating speed. The landslide flung boulders and mud into the air and pulverized everything in its path. Including the town of Yungay. Within seconds, the town was smashed to pieces and the townspeople were buried alive. Altogether, on that one dreadful day, about 60,000 people died.

3 Flaming fires. Without doubt, the most sinister side-effects of earthquakes are flaming fires. Often fire does far more damage than the quake itself. Remember the woman cooking bacon and eggs in San Francisco? The combination of fire and mostly wooden houses turned breakfast into a nightmare. Another tragic case was the city of Lisbon in Portugal. In November 1755, an awesome earthquake hit the city. With devastating results. Large parts of the city lay in ruins. But worse, much worse, was to come. Within a few hours, sparks from overturned cooking stoves and oil lamps had lit a ferocious fire. For three terrible days, the fire swept through the city before, finally, burning itself out. Before the earthquake, Lisbon had been a beautiful place, filled with palaces, fine houses and priceless works of art. Afterwards, it was burned to a crisp. Luckily (for us), the fire was witnessed first hand by a man called Thomas Chase, an Englishman living in Lisbon. Here's what his letter home might have looked like:

Lisbon, Portugal
November 1755

Dearest Mother,

I hope this letter reaches you safely. The post isn't working too well these days. In fact, nothing's working in Lisbon at present. That wretched earthquake's turned our lives upside down. There's not much of the city left. Anyway, I wanted to let you know I'm safe. I'm one of the lucky ones.

I was in my bedroom when the ground started shaking. And there was the most dreadful sound I've ever heard. I knew at once that it was an earthquake. It was gentle at first, then it got stronger and stronger. I'm afraid curiosity got the better of me and I ran to the top of the house for a better look. (I know what you're thinking. Stupid boy! And you're right.) I'd nearly made it when the whole house suddenly lurched sideways and knocked me off my feet. Then I felt myself falling. In fact, I'd been thrown out of a window. (Unfortunately, it was on the fourth floor.) I must have passed out because the next thing I remember was my neighbour dragging me out from under a pile of bricks and rubble. He didn't recognize me at first, I looked such a sight.

Anyway, I was pretty shaken up, I can tell you. My poor body was covered in cuts and bruises, and I'd broken my right arm. (I'm afraid that's why my writing's so shaky.) Someone went and fetched my good friend, Mr Forg, and he took me to his house and put me to bed to recover. At last I was safe. Or so I thought. From my bed, I could spy yellow lights flickering outside the window and I could hear the sickening crackle of flames. Would you believe it, the house was on fire! Brave Mr Forg acted quickly. Twice now he's saved my life. At great personal peril, he carried me to safety in the Square, and there I stayed all Saturday night and Sunday. By now, the whole city was on fire. I wept to see it burning out of control.

As I said, dear Mother, despite my wounds, I was lucky. Although I've lost everything, I still have my life. Many of my friends are much worse off. It has been terrible. Terrible.

Anyway, I'll write again soon. And I may see you even sooner. As soon as I'm better, I'm coming home. Until then, please don't worry about me.

Your loving son,
Thomas

excuse
thumbprint

X X X X X

EARTH-SHATTERING FACT FILE

DATE: 1 November 1755
LOCATION: Lisbon, Portugal
TIME: 9.40 a.m.
LENGTH OF SHOCK: about 3 minutes
MAGNITUDE: 8.7
DEATHS: 60,000
THE SHOCKING FACTS:

• 1 November was All Saints' Day so many people were in church. Many said the earthquake was God's punishment.

• The first tremor was followed by two massive aftershocks.

• An hour and a half after the earthquake, three huge waves rolled in from the sea. Thousands of people drowned.

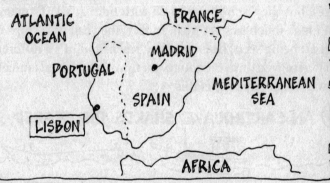

4 Shocking seiches. Spare a thought for the locals who lived around Loch Lochmond in Scotland. They didn't know there'd been an earthquake in Lisbon. (It took two weeks for Britain to get the news.) So when the loch water suddenly started sloshing violently to and fro, they'd absolutely no idea why. What on Earth was going on? Well, this was another seismic side-effect. Its tricky technical name is a seiche (saysh) wave. And it's caused by all those shock waves shooting through the Earth and shaking up the rocks, including the rocks in loch and lake beds.

5 Terrible tsunamis (soo-naa-mees). A tsunami (that's Japanese for "harbour wave") is a gigantic wave triggered off by an earthquake under the sea. Some people call them tidal waves, but they're nothing to do with tides at all. Tsunamis don't look much to start with. In fact, they can pass ships by without being seen. But once they reach land, it's a different story. Are you brave enough to find out how a tsunami grows? What happens is this:

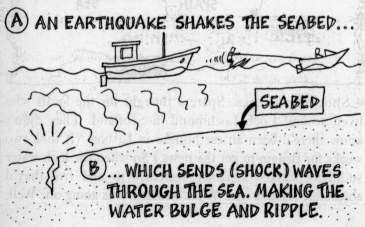

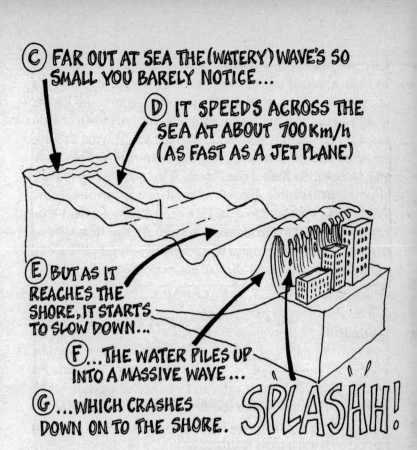

C FAR OUT AT SEA THE (WATERY) WAVE'S SO SMALL YOU BARELY NOTICE...

D IT SPEEDS ACROSS THE SEA AT ABOUT 700 km/h (AS FAST AS A JET PLANE)

E BUT AS IT REACHES THE SHORE, IT STARTS TO SLOW DOWN...

F ...THE WATER PILES UP INTO A MASSIVE WAVE...

G ...WHICH CRASHES DOWN ON TO THE SHORE.

SPLASHH!

Horrible Health Warning...

Tsunamis are horribly dangerous. As they smash on to the shore, they wash everything away. Buildings, boats, people and even WHOLE VILLAGES. Tsunamis can be four times as tall as your house. That's an awful lot of water. Trouble is you don't notice them until it's too late. So if the sea looks as if it's been sucked away from the shore, GET OUT OF THE WAY. FAST! Chances are a tsunami's around the corner, ready to rear its ugly head.

Life-saving early warning

In 1946, a tremor off the coast of Alaska triggered off a series of tsunamis. They sped 3,000 kilometres across the Pacific Ocean all the way to Hawaii. People in the port town of Hilo saw a sheer wall of water rising from the sea. Wave after wave smashed into the harbour, hurling boats and people aside and sweeping whole streets away. The good news is that, after this devastating disaster, a brand-new tsunami warning system was set up. Based in Hawaii, it keeps a round-the-clock earthquake and tsunami watch. At the first sign of trouble, it flashes warnings to stations all around the Pacific, telling people how long they've got to get out of the way. . .

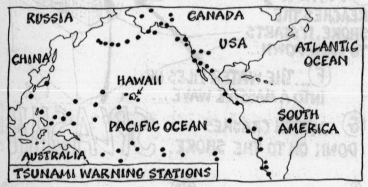

Teacher teaser

Feeling brave? Why not try this sick joke on your geography teacher? Put up your hand and ask:

PLEASE, MISS, WHAT HAPPENED TO THE COW WHO CROSSED THE ROAD IN AN EARTHQUAKE?

Is she ready for the side-splitting reply?

Horrible (Human) Health Warning

Forget crusty plates and restless rocks. Anything that puts the Earth under pressure can trigger off a shock. INCLUDING HORRIBLE HUMANS. One of the worst things humans are doing is filling reservoirs with water. (Reservoirs are like big lakes. They're sometimes used for storing drinking water.) So how on Earth does this set off an earthquake? Well, the weight of the water puts the rocks under serious strain, forcing water down into faults that are already there. In 1967, a massive 6.5 shock hit Koyna in India. The area wasn't known for earthquakes. But, guess what? A brand-new reservoir had just been filled up there.

In future, the numbers of people living on shaky ground is likely to go up and up. After all, quake zones cover large parts of the Earth and you can't avoid them all. Besides, shaking aside, they're often pretty pleasant places to live. So what can be done to make life safer? Time to call the earth-shattering experts in. . .

EARTH-
SHATTERING
EXPERT!

EARTHQUAKE EXPERTS

Scientists who study earth-shattering earthquakes are called seismologists (size–moll–ow–gists). And no, their name's got nothing to do with the size of their brains. Though they'd probably like you to think so. Forget pictures of batty professors in long, white coats snoozing away in dusty laboratories. Seismologists are scientists under pressure. Their tricky task is to work out what makes awesome earthquakes tick. But it isn't as simple as it sounds. Earthquakes are horribly unpredictable. No one knows where and when the next quake will hit. Does this put the stressed-out seismologists off? No way. It just makes them keener than ever to crack on and break new ground.

Could you be a seismologist?

Do you have what it takes to be a seismologist? Would you be able to stand the strain? Try this quick quiz to find out. Better still, try it out on your geography teacher.

1 Are you a whizz at maths? Yes/No

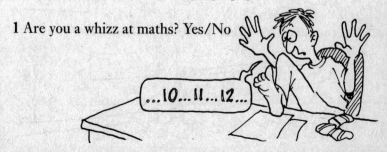

2 Fabulous at physics? Yes/No

3 Marvellous at map-reading? Yes/No

4 Have you got a good imagination? Yes/No

5 Have you got eyes in the back of your head? Yes/No

6 Do you fancy travelling to exotic locations? Yes/No

Answers:

1 You'll need to be. A lot of seismology means collecting scientific information and feeding it into computers. Then working out what on Earth it all means. How do you do this? By doing horribly long and complicated sums, that's how. So you need to be pretty nifty with numbers.

2 Physics is useful for finding out how shock waves travel through the Earth. Unfortunately, shock waves don't go in nice, straight lines. That would be too easy. So plotting their path from A (the earthquake's epicentre) to B (the surface of the ground) isn't nice and straightforward either. As they pass through different types of soil or rock, the wayward waves get reflected back on themselves or bent at an angle (technically speaking, bending's called refraction). Either way, it sends them speeding off in all directions. And guess what? Yep, reflection and refraction are bits of physics.

3 If you get lost finding your way to school (especially if it's geography test day), a map won't help you much. But if you're really serious about seismology, map-reading's a must. I mean, how else will you spot the shock?

4 No, I don't mean imagining things like your teacher telling you you're a genius. That really would be a dream come true. This is the sort of imagination that lets you think up a 3-D picture of what's inside the Earth. Without actually being able to see it. It's essential because this is where earthquakes actually happen. But it's tricky because there aren't any maps. It's a bit like you trying to find that bag of crisps you know you hid under your bed, IN THE DARK.

HMM! STILL TASTY AFTER SIX MONTH'S

5 Of course, you don't really need eyes in the back of your head. (Think of the fortune you'd have to spend in cool sunshades!) But you do need to be observant.

So are you on the ball or would you sleep through anything? Try filling in this real-life earthquake questionnaire. It's for finding out how you'd react in an earthquake. Even if you've never lived through a real-life earthquake, think about how you might answer the questions if you had.

EARTHQUAKE QUESTIONNAIRE

1. Where were you when the earthquake happened?

2. What time was the tremor?

3. Did you feel any vibrations?

4. What did you hear?

5. Were you indoors or out?

6. Were you sitting/standing/lying down/active/ sleeping/listening to the radio/watching TV?

7. Were you frightened?

8. Did any doors or windows rattle?

9. Did anything else rattle?

10. Did any hanging objects swing?

11. Did anything fall?

12. Was there any damage?

---

6 You'll have the chance to visit seismic stations all around the world in such unusual places as the Arctic, the Antarctic, the Himalayas, Africa and New Zealand. Better get your atlas out!

How do you think you'd do?

Snapshots of the stars

Don't worry if seismology's got you stumped. Sit back and let the real earthquake experts take the strain. Are you ready to rub shoulders with some of the most shockingly clever scientists ever? Here's Sid to introduce you to five real brainboxes. . .

NAME: John Michell
(1724 - 1793)
NATIONALITY: British

CLAIM TO FAME: Professor of geology at Cambridge University. In 1760 John published the first scientific paper on earthquakes after studying the disastrous Lisbon quake. (The paper was called "Conjectures Concerning the Cause and Observations upon the Phenomena of Earthquakes", in case you were wondering. Unfortunately, it was so horribly boring that not many people bothered to read it.) Still, brainy John was nicknamed the "father of seismology" for his ground-breaking work. He realized that waves travelled at different speeds and worked out a way of finding earthquake epicentres. As if that wasn't enough, in his spare time he was a top astronomer. What a swot.

NAME: Robert Mallet
(1810 - 1881)
NATIONALITY: Irish

CLAIM TO FAME: Robert got hooked on earthquakes by accident. By training, he was an engineer. He designed railway stations, bridges and lighthouses. All this changed one day, when he read about earthquakes in a book. From then on, Robert became an earthquake bore. Instead of stamps, he collected earthquake books, pamphlets, newspaper articles. . . You name it, he'd collect it. (He even made his own earthquakes, by exploding gunpowder underground. He had to, you see, because he lived in Ireland, far away from any earthquake zones.) Then he put the whole lot together in a massive book. And that wasn't all. He plotted the biggest earthquakes on a map. And get this. Mallet's map was so amazingly accurate, it's still used today.

NAME: Andrija Mohorovicic
(1857 - 1936)
NATIONALITY: Croatian

CLAIM TO FAME: Andrija worked out that earthquakes happen in the Earth's crust. But he found that some of the shock waves shoot through the mantle. The boundary between the crust and mantle was named the Mohorovicic discontinuity, after him.

Thankfully, it was such a mouthful, it's now been shortened to Moho. Anyway, Moho was a real clever clogs. Not only was he brilliant at physics and maths, geology and meteorology, he also spoke fluent Croatian, English, French, Italian, Latin, Greek and Czech. So he could say "earthquake" in seven different languages! If he'd wanted to.

NAME: Beno Gutenberg
(1889-1960)
NATIONALITY: American

CLAIM TO FAME: Gutenberg spent years studying seismic waves and working out how they travelled. He also helped Charles Richter work out the, er, Richter scale. (So strictly speaking that should have been the Gutenberg-Richter scale.) Again with his pal Richter, Beno showed that three-quarters of earthquakes happen around the shaky Pacific Ocean. But you knew that already. Brainy Beno's best-known books included Earthquakes of North America and The Seismicity of the Earth. OK, I know they sound too boring to read.

NAME: John Milne (1850-1913)
NATIONALITY: British

CLAIM TO FAME: Brilliant John Milne really shook things up by inventing the first practical seismograph (size-mow-graf). That's a posh bit of equipment for measuring earthquakes. Here's the amazing true story of his shocking discovery. . .

A shocking discovery

John Milne was born in Liverpool, England. He trained at the Royal School of Mines in London and became a mining engineer. (That's someone in charge of building mines underground. Sounds boring – gettit? – but someone had to do it.) When John was just 25 years old, he was offered the job of a lifetime. He became professor of geology and mining at the Imperial College of Engineering in Tokyo, Japan. Posh, or what?

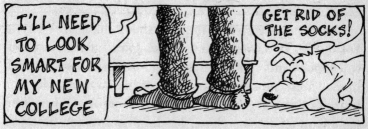

I'LL NEED TO LOOK SMART FOR MY NEW COLLEGE

GET RID OF THE SOCKS!

There was just one teeny little snag. . . Japan was a very long way from Liverpool and John hated the sea. (Which was strange for someone who loved to travel. As a young man he was always on the move.) Instead he went most of the way overland, through Europe and Russia. It took 11 long, tiring months to reach Japan. And to make matters worse, on John's very first night in his new home, Tokyo was struck by a (small-ish) earthquake! What a shock! And it wouldn't be John's last. As you know, Japan stands on horribly shaky ground. John later wrote that there were earthquakes "for breakfast, dinner, supper and to sleep on". But for the time being, he had other things on his mind. His new job kept him on his toes. Especially the bit where he had to climb to the tops of active volcanoes to inspect their fiery craters. Luckily, the volcanoes didn't blow their tops else daring John would have been a goner. Then who knows what seismologists would have done.

In 1880 a powerful earthquake shook the nearby city of Yokohama. It was enough to make John turn his back on volcanoes and concentrate on earthquakes instead. Immediately, he called a meeting of like-minded scientists and set up the Seismological Society of Japan. (When John put his mind to something, he didn't waste any time you see.) From then on, there was no stopping him. Studying earthquakes became his life's work. But first he needed to find out more about them. The question was how? Then clever John had a brainwave. He needed information and he needed it fast. (And people didn't have telephones or the internet then.) So he sent every post office for miles around a bundle of stamped, self-addressed postcards. All the postmaster (or mistress) had to do was fill in one card every week and post it back to John, describing any tremors. They didn't even need to buy a stamp. Pretty cunning, eh? What's more, it worked! Soon John was swamped with mail bags. There were postcards everywhere. From the answers he got, he was able to draw up detailed maps of every single shock and shudder to shake Japan.

DEAR JOHN, HAVING A LOVELY TIME, WEATHER GREAT...

But John still wasn't satisfied. Eyewitness accounts were all very well but you couldn't really rely on them. People were always exaggerating or playing things down. For example, you might accidentally tick the answer "huge" to describe the size of a tremor, when all along you meant "quite small" but you didn't want your postcard to look dead boring. Anyway, what John desperately needed was a posh machine for measuring earthquakes accurately. Various ingenious instruments had been invented but none of them worked very well. Did John give up? Did he, heck. No, he went and invented one of his own. The instrument was called a seismograph (size-mow-graf). It recorded the shock waves from an earthquake so scientists could study and measure them. When an earthquake struck and shook the seismograph, a pin or pen traced the pattern of shaking on to a piece of smoked paper or glass. It was brilliant. Earth-shatteringly brilliant.

Getting the shakes

Basic seismographs haven't changed much since John Milne's time. Which just shows how bloomin' brainy he was. But how on Earth do these marvellous machines work? Do you need to be a genius geographer to use one? Or is it something even your teacher could grasp? Who better to guide you through the muddle than Sid's very own Uncle Stan, the handyman.

MORNIN', STAN HERE. NOW WHAT'S THIS ABOUT SEISMOGRAPHS? PESKY THINGS, I AGREE. NEVER MIND, YOU STICK WITH ME AND WE'LL SOON HAVE THE BEAUTY UP AND RUNNING. FIRST YOU NEED TO GET TO KNOW HOW ALL THE BITS AND PIECES WORK.

Your Seismograph...

frame (fixed to the ground)

heavy weight

spring

squiggly pattern

shaking Earth

rotating roll of paper

scratchy pen

STAN'S TOP TIP: Don't worry if your seismograph doesn't look exactly like this one. There are lots of different types. Some use a beam of light to trace the pattern on to photographic film. Others record the wave pattern electronically or digitally. (The last ones are probably best left to the experts, in my view.)

HOW IT WORKS...

WHEN THE GROUND SHAKES, THE FRAME SHAKES TOO, THIS SHAKES THE ROLL OF PAPER, THE WEIGHT DOESN'T MOVE, SO THE PEN FIXED TO IT SCRATCHES A PATTERN ON THE PAPER.

Checking the print-out

The posh technical term for the squiggly lines on the paper is a seismogram (size–mow–gram). Oh they like making things difficult, these scientists. The squiggles show the shock waves from an earthquake. The bigger the squiggles, the bigger the quake. Still with me? Good. Now you've just got to decipher your seismogram, and you're home and dry.

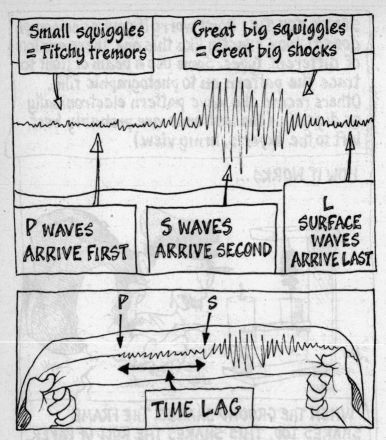

Small squiggles = Titchy tremors

Great big squiggles = Great big shocks

P WAVES ARRIVE FIRST

S WAVES ARRIVE SECOND

L SURFACE WAVES ARRIVE LAST

P

S

TIME LAG

The size of the waves is used to work out the earthquake's magnitude. The closer the earthquake, the bigger the waves.

STAN'S TOP TIP: For more accurate readings, try burying your seismograph underground. I've done that with quite a few of mine. But don't forget to check it regularly. If you can remember where to dig...

Worldwide watch

For many years, John Milne continued his earth-shattering studies. Then in 1895 disaster struck. Fire broke out and destroyed John's home and his precious observatory. Luckily, John and his wife escaped unhurt but his priceless collection of books and instruments went up in smoke. Years of hard work were lost in minutes. Shattered, John left Japan and returned to England, but he didn't stop his earthquake watch. In his new home, on the Isle of Wight, he built himself a brand-new observatory, complete with a brand-new seismograph. It was the first of many. By 1902, he'd set up similar observatories all over the world to keep a 24-hour eye on earthquakes.

Today, the Worldwide Standardized Seismic Network (WSSN, for short) has monitoring stations all over the world, measuring earthquakes as they happen. Using the latest high-tech seismographs, they can pinpoint the epicentre of a major quake in just 15 minutes. And sound the alarm. . .

Earth-shattering fact

The first ever seismograph was invented in China in about AD 130. It was built by Zhang Heng, a brilliant mathematician, astronomer, map-maker, painter, poet, and, er, seismograph-maker. (Don't some people make you sick?) But it didn't look like any seismograph you'd see today. It was a big bronze vase ringed with bronze dragons and toads. Each dragon held a bronze ball in its mouth. Inside the vase hung a heavy pendulum. When the Earth shook, the pendulum tilted, making the dragon furthest from the earthquake's epicentre drop its ball. Did this convoluted contraption work? Incredibly, it did!

Teacher teaser

If you're thinking of taking up seismology seriously, you'll need more than a seismograph. Why not baffle your teacher with the names of some other impressive-sounding instruments. Try this one for starters:

What on Earth are you talking about?

Answer: A creepmeter's a useful instrument for measuring how much the ground moves along a fault just before an earthquake. (And has nothing to do with being a creepy swot and giving your teacher apples.) If your creepmeter's really on the blink, you could be in for a bumpy ride. To be a real earthquake expert, you might need a strainmeter and a tiltmeter too. A strainmeter measures how much the rocks are squeezed or stretched. A tiltmeter works out how much the ground, er, tilts. Oh, so you knew that already!

If you're itching to get out and get on with your measuring (are you raving mad?), don't go just yet. Your seismograph might be up and running but it can only get the measure of an earthquake AFTER THE EARTHQUAKE'S OVER. It can't tell you where a quake might happen next. So before you go charging off, read the next chapter. Please. It might be a matter of life and death.

SHOCKING WARNING SIGNS

Never mind fancy instruments with fine-sounding names. What if your new-fangled seismograph breaks down under the strain? Then you'd be in serious trouble. Besides, earth-shattering earthquakes are so horribly hard to predict, seismologists need all the extra help they can get. So how on Earth can you tell if and when an earthquake's about to strike? Is it even possible? Could you spot the shocking warning signs?

OOOOOOH! EARTHQUAKE

Could you be a seismologist?
The ground starts shaking and you're scared stiff. You run into the street, just before your house collapses behind you. You've lost everything, your best trainers, your precious collection of computer games. But you're lucky to be alive. If only you'd known to expect an earthquake. Then you could have grabbed your belongings and got out of there, fast. Are there any warning signs you could have looked out for? Take a look at the clues below. Seismologists think they may be tell-tale signs of stress. Tick the box if you see them.

1 Weird water. Weird things happen to water just before earthquakes. For months or even years before, water levels in wells get lower and lower. Then, suddenly, the water shoots back up again. Other watery signs include foaming lakes, boiling seas and fountains that won't stop flowing. See if you notice anything strange next time you have a bath. (Remember the bath? It's that big tub thing in the bathroom?)

2 Gushing geysers. Geysers are gigantic jets of steam and scalding water that's heated to boiling point by hot rocks underground. Then it bursts into the air. You could set your watch by certain geysers. Take Old Faithful in California, USA. It usually erupts every 40 minutes. Regular as clockwork. Except before an earthquake, that is. Then the gap doubles to two hours or more. Scientists aren't sure why this happens but they're not taking any chances. They've got a computer watching this gushing geyser 24 hours a day.

TICK IF YOU'VE SPOTTED

OL' FAITHFUL

EARTHQUAKE WEEKLY

TICK IF YOU'VE SPOTTED

3 Ghastly gases. Radon is a ghastly gas given off by underground rocks. It seeps to the surface in springs and stream water. Before an earthquake, scientists have noticed that the seeping starts to speed up. It seems that stressed-out rocks release more radon. This is exactly what happened just before the 1995 Kobe quake. Unfortunately, the warning signs were ignored.

4 Frightful foreshocks. Before a big quake you often get lots of little mini-quakes. Seismologists call them foreshocks. They get bigger and stronger as the stress builds up. And they're pretty good clues, *if* they happen. Trouble is you sometimes don't feel any foreshocks at all. Not even the tiniest tremble. Or if you do, they may just fizzle out again, without doing any damage.

DID YOU HAVE BEANS FOR LUNCH?

TICK IF YOU'VE SPOTTED

DID YOU FEEL THAT SMALL TREMBLE, JUST THEN?

TICK IF YOU'VE SPOTTED

5 Bright lights. If the sky fills with fireworks (and it's not 5 November yet), watch out. An earthquake might be around the corner. An hour before the Kobe quake, people saw flashes of red, green and blue light streaking across the sky. The tricky technical name for this is fractoluminescence (frakto–loom–in–essence) which means broken lights. Scientists think the lights are caused by smashed–up bits of sparkly quartz, a crusty crystal found in rocks.

TICK IF YOU'VE SPOTTED

6 Stormy weather. For years, people believed in "earthquake weather". Trouble is, they couldn't agree what it was. Some said it was calm weather with clear, blue skies. Others said it was stormy weather with frightening lightning and pouring rain. Who was right? Neither, I'm afraid. You can blame the weather for lots of things, like not being able to go out on your bike. But you can't blame it for earthquakes.

TICK IF YOU'VE SPOTTED

How many warning signs did you spot? Hopefully, you won't have ticked anything. Which means you're perfectly safe and sound, and don't need to worry.

Alarming animals

If you don't think any of these warnings would work, don't worry. Try some old-fashioned folklore instead. Some people say animals start acting oddly before earthquakes. Scientists think animals may be reacting to very high-pitched sounds that we can't hear, coming from tiny cracks around the area that's about to quake. So watch out if your pet cat *stops* chasing mice or your pet dog *starts* purring. You may be in for a nasty shock. Which of the following wildlife warning signs are too way-out to be true?

a) Catfish wriggle and leap out of water. TRUE/FALSE?

b) Rats panic and run away. TRUE/FALSE

c) Pet dogs and cats go missing. TRUE/FALSE?

d) Wild animals like tigers behave like, er, pussycats. TRUE/FALSE?

e) Honey bees abandon their hives? TRUE/FALSE?

f) Worms worm their way to the surface? TRUE/FALSE?

g) Crocodiles lose their cool. TRUE/FALSE?

h) Goldfish go mad and jump out of their bowls. TRUE/FALSE?

Answers: Incredibly, they're all TRUE. But what on Earth sends these animals into such a spin? Well, it might be because they can hear very low rumbling sounds coming from the Earth. Too low for human ears to hear. Or they might sense changes in the Earth's magnetic field (the Earth's insides act like a very weak magnet). One thing's for certain. Woe betide those spoilsport scientists who tell you it's all a load of nonsense. They'd better not mess with a cross crocodile. Or they might end up as its lunch!

Cracking clues or pure coincidence?

So do any of these warning signs *really* work? Are they crucial quake-busting clues? Or just amazing coincidences? To tell you the truth, there's no easy answer. Sometimes they work. And sometimes they don't work. In the shaky world of seismology, you can't rely on anything. As you're about to find out when you read these two shocking true stories. . .

Lucky escape

On 4 February 1975 an earth-shattering earthquake struck the city of Haicheng in China. But instead of thousands of deaths (90,000 people lived in the city), only 300 people lost their lives. It could have been worse. Much worse. But for several months before the quake hit, people started noticing weird warnings signs. Hibernating snakes woke up suddenly and slithered sleepily out of their holes, even though it was still winter and they weren't meant to wake up until the spring. Groups of rats were seen running round in circles. What's more, there were 500 foreshocks in the space of three days. It all added up to a massive shock. Fortunately, the authorities decided to take notice of these warning signs. They couldn't predict exactly when an earthquake might strike, but they weren't prepared to take any chances. Finally, at 2 p.m. on 4 February, the city was evacuated. People got ready to spend the freezing night outdoors in tents and straw shelters. Five and a half hours later, at 7.36 p.m., the earthquake struck. . . It measured 7.3 on the Richter scale. The evacuation had come in the nick of time.

Total disaster
But had the warnings signs done the trick? Could they really be relied on? Many seismologists dismissed the prediction as a fluke. True, thousands of lives had been saved. But it could have been a lucky guess. Were they right? Eighteen months later, at 3.43 a.m. on 28 July 1976, another Chinese city was struck by another awesome earthquake. This quake measured 7.8 on the Richter scale. But the people of

Tangshan weren't so lucky. There were no warning signs whatsoever. No startled snakes. No rattled rats. No rumbling foreshocks. Nothing. In little over a minute, more than 300,000 people were killed. Thousands more were badly injured. The city itself was completely demolished. It was one of the most devastating earthquakes ever. And nobody saw it coming. . .

Can we really predict earthquakes?

Will earthquakes ever be properly predicted? Can seismologists ever hope to stay one step ahead? Horribly simple questions, you might think. Horribly simple questions . . . with impossibly tricky answers. So tricky that even the earth-shattering experts can't agree. Just listen to these two, for starters. . .

No! It's not like forecasting the weather, you know. We can't give nice, precise predictions. I mean, we can't say an earthquake of a certain size will strike a certain place at a certain time. It's not like saying it'll rain in Spain next Tuesday. (Not that weather forecasts are always right.) It simply isn't possible. We just don't know enough about the Earth's insides. Besides, some earthquakes strike without any warning. So there's no way of telling they're even on their way.

Yes! We can give very general warnings. We can say a place can expect a big earthquake sometime this century. But we can't say exactly when or where. It's all down to probability. A bit like you saying you might get round to doing your homework sometime this week. Not horribly exact, is it? But we can pinpoint possible danger zones on a map. So people have time to prepare. OK, it's not much. But it's better than nothing.

If seismologists could even give 20 seconds' (yes, *seconds*) warning, they could save thousands of lives. But scientists have to be careful. A false alarm could be fatal. If they order an evacuation, and no earthquake hits, people might not be so keen to listen next time. Even if they could predict an earthquake, of course, they couldn't do anything to stop it happening. And that's the only thing they know for certain!

SURVIVING THE SHOCK

OK, so your pet cat's left home. DON'T PANIC. Your cat's most likely off chasing mice. It's very, very unlikely that this means an earthquake's about to strike. But you never know. So what would you do if the Earth suddenly shattered? How would you cope? No idea? Luckily Sid's here with his earth-shattering guide to earthquake survival. Don't go to bed without it. . .

Earth-shattering earthquake survival guide

Hi, Sid here. If you live in a quake zone, it pays to be prepared. Better safe than sorry, I always say. Places used to earth-shattering earthquakes practise regular earthquake drills. They're a bit like the fire drills you have at school, except you don't have to spend hours standing in the playground in the soaking rain. Thank goodness. Anyway, to practise staying safe in an earthquake, here are some essential dos and don'ts:

DO. . .

- **Stock up on supplies.** Pack an emergency survival kit. You'll need a fire extinguisher, a torch (with spare batteries), a first-aid kit, tinned food (don't forget a tin-opener and food for your cat – he's bound to come home in the end), bottled water (enough for three days), sleeping bags or blankets, warm clothes and sturdy shoes (for walking over rubble and broken glass). Keep these things somewhere handy and make sure everyone in your family or class knows where they are.

- **Listen to the radio.** Keep a radio (and more spare batteries) in your emergency kit. After the quake, communications may be cut for several days or even weeks. So stay in touch by tuning in to your radio for information and advice.

- **Be prepared.** Make sure everyone in your family or class knows what to do. (Practise beforehand.) Fix up a meeting place for after the quake in case you get split up.

- **Turn off the gas and electricity.** The quake may break gas pipes and snap power lines. So you'll need your torch for seeing in the dark. Never, ever light a match. If there's been a gas leak, everything could go up in flames.

- **Crouch under a sturdy table.** Or under your desk if you're at school. Cover your head with a cushion or pillow, and press your face into your arm. This'll protect your head and eyes from broken glass and flying objects. Hold on tight to the table leg. Now don't move until the shaking stops. Remember, DUCK, COVER AND HOLD ON. (If you're not near a table, stand in a doorway. Doorframes are pretty strong.)

DON'T….
- **Rush outside.** Wait until the house stops shaking before you rush outside. Otherwise you might get hit by flying glass or debris. (Or you might fall out of a window. Remember poor Thomas Chase?) The general rule is: if you're inside, stay inside and if you're outside, stay put.

- **Use the stairs.** If you live in a block of flats, or you're at school, stay away from the stairs. At least until the shaking's stopped. You could easily fall or get crushed. Whatever happens, don't use the lift. If the power's cut, you'll be trapped.

- **Stand by a building.** Once the shaking's stopped and you can go outside, find an open space to stand in. Stay away from buildings, trees, chimneys, power lines, and anything that might fall on top of you.

- **Go for a drive.** At least, not until the shaking's over. If you're in a car, slow down and stop in an open space. But watch out for falling rocks and landslides. And don't go anywhere near a bridge. It'll probably collapse with you on top. Stay inside the car until the shaking's stopped.

- **Use the phone.** For the first few days after the earthquake, don't use the phone. If it's really, really urgent, OK. But don't phone your friends for a chat. It might clog up the phone lines and stop emergency calls getting through.

Earthquake rescue

Phew! You've made it. But you've been lucky. In the chaos that follows a major earthquake, thousands of people may be injured or killed. Many are buried under collapsed buildings. Leaving the rescue teams with no time to lose. But it's a horribly risky job. At any moment, a building could come crashing down on top of the rescuers, especially if small aftershocks hit it. Besides, they may only have tools like pick-axes, spades, or even their bare hands to work with. Even with the latest high-tech equipment, like cameras that detect body heat and listening devices, it's a race against time. (Specially trained dogs are also used. Not so high-tech but brilliant at sniffing out survivors.) The rescuers know they have to work fast. Without much air or water, trapped victims may only have days to live. For some people, help arrives too late if it arrives at all. But it isn't all bad news. Sometimes, somehow, against all the odds, miracles do happen. Take the extraordinary events in Mexico City. . .

EARTH-SHATTERING FACT FILE

DATE: 19 September 1985
LOCATION: Mexico City, Mexico
TIME: 7.18 a.m.
LENGTH OF SHOCK: 3 minutes
MAGNITUDE: 8.1
DEATH TOLL: 10,000
THE SHOCKING FACTS:

• The epicentre was 400 km away, off the coast. It took a minute for the shock waves to reach the city.
• Thirty-six hours later a second massive shock struck. It measured 7.5 on the Richter scale.
• The city centre was hardest hit with thousands of buildings damaged and destroyed.

The Daily Globe 🌐

29 September 1985, Mexico City

MIRACLE BABIES IN RESCUE SHOCK

Ten days after a massive earthquake devastated the city, rescuers are celebrating a miracle. Two new-born babies have been pulled alive from the ruins of the maternity hospital. A doctor who examined the babies told our reporter, "It's wonderful news. Babies are pretty tough, you know. When they suffer a really big shock, they're able to slow their bodies right down. It's like animals hibernating. That way, they can stay alive for a surprisingly long time without food or water."

OH, BABY!

The babies had a very lucky escape. The multi-storey hospital in which they were born collapsed like a house of cards. Its twisted remains are all that are left. About a thousand doctors, nurses and patients were buried under the rubble.

TOTAL COLLAPSE

PET RESCUE

It's the same story all over the city. Since the quake struck, exhausted rescuers have worked around the clock to pull survivors out. As the days wear on, their task becomes even grimmer. Now there are mainly dead bodies to bring out. But finding the babies has given the rescuers a much-needed boost. One man told us, with tears in his eyes, "It's like a beacon of hope in all the misery and blackness. We'd almost given up hope of finding anyone else alive. These little ones have given us the strength we needed to carry on with our efforts."

Quake-proof construction

In an earth-shattering earthquake, it's not shock that kills
people but collapsing buildings. So what can be done to cut
the risk? Well, architects and engineers are already working
on the problem. They're trying to build quake-proof
buildings that can really stand the strain.

BUILDERS FOR HIRE

HOUSE STARTING TO SWAY?

WALLS STARTING TO CRACK?

NEED QUAKE-PROOFING YOU CAN RELY ON?

LOOK NO FURTHER...

SACKED

RUMBLE, CRUMBLE, TUMBLE & SONS BUILDERS

LET US TAKE THE STRAIN

SMALL PRINT: DON'T BLAME US IF YOUR HOUSE FALLS DOWN. WITH EARTHQUAKES
THERE ARE NO GUARANTEES. QUAKE-PROOFING MIGHT DO THE TRICK.
THEN AGAIN, IT MIGHT NOT. SORRY.

115

Want to make sure your house survives the shock and stays standing? But daren't trust the small ads? Why not do it yourself? Sneak a look in this dusty but helpful DIY manual to find out what you need to do. And if you can't tell one end of a hammer from the other, don't worry. Here's Sid's Uncle Stan back to help you with more of his handy hints and tips.

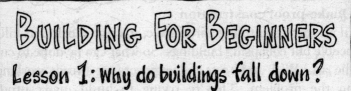

BUILDING FOR BEGINNERS

Lesson 1: Why do buildings fall down?

Before you learn how to keep your house standing up, you need to find out why it might fall down. Are you brave enough to shake your house down?

WHAT YOU NEED:

- A SMALL PLASTIC BOTTLE OF ORANGE SQUASH* (FOR THE HOUSE)

- A PIECE OF CARD (FOR THE EARTH)

WHAT TO DO:

① PLACE THE BOTTLE ON THE CARD

② PUSH THE CARD SLOWLY BACKWARDS AND FORWARDS

③ DO THIS AGAIN REALLY QUICKLY THIS TIME

④ DO THIS AGAIN AT A SPEED SOMEWHERE BETWEEN THE TWO

What happens?

a) The bottle shakes a bit but doesn't fall over.
b) The bottle sways but doesn't fall over.
c) The bottle sways a lot and falls over.

Answer: It depends how fast you push the card. If you push slowly, the bottle wobbles a bit but doesn't fall over. If you push quickly, it sways at the top but still stays up. But if you push at a speed somewhere between the two, the bottle falls over. This is because it's shaking at exactly the same frequency** as the card. It's the same when an earthquake strikes. If a building shakes at exactly the same frequency as the ground, it soon topples over.

* You can drink the squash when you've finished this chapter. DIY can be thirsty work. Don't use fizzy pop though. It'll spurt all over the place when you open the bottle and make a terrible mess.

** Frequency's the tricky technical term for the number of shock waves passing through it each second.

STAN'S HANDY HINTS NO. 1

Pick the shape carefully when you're planning your house. Take a look at these two barmy buildings. Which one do you think would work best in an earthquake?

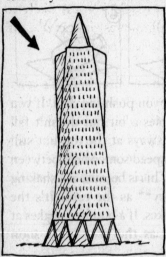

GIVE UP? IN FACT, THEY BOTH WORK BRILLIANTLY. THE PYRAMID SHAPE, ON THE LEFT, IS GREAT IN AN EARTHQUAKE. THIS PARTICULAR BUILDING'S IN SAN FRANCISCO. IN THE 1989 LOMA PRIETA QUAKE, ITS 49 STOREYS SWAYED A BIT BUT DIDN'T FALL DOWN. THE BEEHIVE SHAPE, ON THE RIGHT, IS ANOTHER CRACKING DESIGN. IT'S SHORT AND SQUAT AND KEEPS ITS FEET FIRMLY ON THE GROUND.

LESSON 2: STOPPING THE SHAKING

OK, so now you know why buildings fall down in an earthquake. But how can you keep them standing? The first thing you've got to do is cut down the shaking. If your house doesn't shake so much, it's less likely to tumble. There's a range of techniques you can use. All tried and tested by yours truly. You could. . .

• **Fit shock absorbers.** Shock absorbers are giant rubber pads used to soak up shock waves. Build them into a wall and you'll cut down the shaking. They've even been used on the Golden Gate Bridge in shaky San Francisco. If another quake strikes, they'll stop the roadway smashing into the towers and bringing the whole lot down. (With any luck.)

• **Make it some sandwiches.** No, not the sort you get filled with cheese or tuna fish. These sandwiches are made from thick layers of rubber and steel. Fancy sinking your chops into one? Fix the sandwiches to your building's foundations. They'll hold it up *and* stop it shaking.

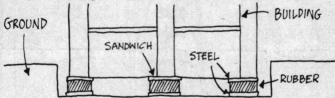

• **Weigh it down.** Some high-rise buildings have heavy weights at the top. You could call them top-heavy, ha! ha! The weights are worked electronically. When a quake hits, they rock in the opposite direction to the shaking. Balancing it out. Brilliant, eh? But horribly expensive. If you're short of cash, they're not for you.

QUICK, RUN OVER TO THE OTHER SIDE!

• **Put up some wallpaper.** That's right, wallpaper. But not the flowery stuff you get at your granny's. This is wallpaper like never before. And your granny would *hate* it. It looks like a roll of shiny black plastic. You paste it on and leave it to dry. Just like ordinary wallpaper. But there's nothing ordinary about this stuff. When it's dry, it's 17 times harder than steel! That's seriously tough stuff. So instead of your wall cracking up, the seismic super-paper holds it all together.

• **Clear out the garage.** If you're thinking of building a garage under your house, think again. Large spaces like garages make the ground floor horribly unstable. If you've already got a garage, clear all the junk out (actually this bit's not essential but your parents will be pleased), then fix the garage to the foundations with giant springs. They'll bend with the shock, then ping back into place once the shaking's over. Leaving your house standing.

STAN'S HANDY HINTS NO. 2

The best material to build with is something that gives, like wood or reinforced concrete (that's concrete strengthened with steel). Something that'll bend a bit. Don't use brittle bricks or hollow concrete blocks. They'll break if the quake's a big 'un. I'd also use shatter-resistant glass, if I were you.

LESSON 3: TESTING YOUR BUILDING

Right, it's crunch time. You've quake-proofed your house but will it stand up? Until it feels the full force of a real-life earthquake, you can't really tell. But a real-life earthquake's the last thing you want. So what on Earth do you do? Here's what the experts suggest:

1 First, build a model of your house. It doesn't need to be exactly the same size. A scaled-down version will do.

2 Next, find a shake-table. No, a table with a wobbly leg won't do. This is a high-tech bit of equipment for testing out buildings in earthquake conditions. They're horribly expensive so you might need to borrow one from the experts.

THANKS FOR LENDING ME YOUR TABLE, SHAKE.

YES, IT DOES

3 Place your model on the table. Then make the table shake. (Note: you don't need to do the shaking yourself. A computer will do it for you. They're specially programmed to do just that.)

BANANA SHAKE

4 Stand back and watch what happens. If your house falls down, start again. (And this time, make sure you follow all the instructions.) If your house stays up, congratulations. You're obviously a whizz at seismic DIY.

STAN'S HANDY HINTS NO.3

It's a good idea to fix wardrobes and bookcases to the wall, so they don't fall on top of you during an earthquake. Fix latches on your kitchen cupboards. The last thing you want is flying tins of baked beans. If you can't find the fixings you need, try a company called Quake Busters in California. (Yes, it's a real company!) I've heard they'll fix anything.

LESSON 4: CHOOSING YOUR SITE

Be careful where you build your house. Some types of ground are shakier than others. Don't choose a spot where the ground's horribly soggy or soft. You'd be asking for trouble. When this type of soil's shaken up, the water in it rises to the surface, turning the soil to jelly. You won't get a building to stand up in that. I mean, have you ever tried standing a spoon in a bowl of wobbly jelly?

This is what happened to Mexico City in 1985. The city's built on a dried-out lake bed. A very bad move indeed. When the earthquake hit, the lake bed turned to jelly. Some buildings sank straight into the ground. Others tilted over on their sides. To make matters worse, the lake bed's shaped like a bowl. So what, you might ask? Well, the shape made the shock waves bigger and stronger. Which made the damage and devastation many, many times worse.

So what type of ground is best to build on? Somewhere nice and rock-solid would do.

STAN'S HANDY HINTS NO. 4...

Make sure you follow the local building code. Most quake-prone cities have one. Trouble is, quake-proofing's a seriously costly business. And some builders cut costs by breaking the rules. Instead of proper materials, they'll use cheaper, shoddier stuff, turning their buildings into killers. Besides, in poor countries, many people can't afford to live in posh, quake-proofed buildings. So they end up living in death-traps instead. It's a very tricky problem.

Shocking, isn't it? But it isn't all doom and gloom. All over the world, seismologists, architects and engineers are working hard to make shaky cities safer. Will they succeed? Who knows? The only way they can really put their new buildings to the test is to wait for the next earthquake. . .

A SHAKY FUTURE?

So is the future set to get shakier? Or will earthquakes soon be a thing of the past? Let's go back to our stressed-out seismologists and see what they have to say. Oh, dear, they're *still* squabbling. . .

If you think things have got off to a shaky start, watch out! They're set to get even shakier. The Big One could strike at any time. And, believe me, it'll be a megaquake. Where will it strike? Hard to tell. Chances are it'll be along a fault. A fault that's been nice and quiet for centuries. A fault where the strain's been building up and up, until suddenly it reaches breaking point. The Big One's already long overdue. Help! Help! Is there a table I can hide under?

Don't listen, it may never happen. Earthquakes aren't any more frequent than they used to be. It's just that more of them hit the headlines. And we scientists have got more sensitive seismographs so we can spot the small ones more easily. It might be ages before we can predict earthquakes accurately. If we ever can. But we're finding out lots more about them. So, even if we can't beat them just yet, we can learn to live with them. Pssst! You can come out from under the table now!

So you see, even the experts don't know for certain. But don't go digging up the playground just yet to see if *your* school's on shaky ground. (It *won't* get you out of double geography. Shame on you!) It's more likely your teacher will come down on you like a tonne of bricks for reading this book in class than you'll be shaken up by an earthquake. Of course with earthquakes you never know what shocks are in store, do you? You'll just have to wait and see. And that, I'm afraid, is the earth-shattering truth!

If you're still interested in finding out more, here are some seismic websites to visit:

http://www.iris.edu
The Incorporated Research Institutes for Seismology. With posters, web pages, maps and photos.

http://www.gsrg.nmh.ac.uk
The British Geological Survey's website, with up-to-date lists and maps of UK earthquakes.

http://www.earthquake.usgs.gov
The US Geological Survey. Maps, lists, facts and figures of earthquakes in the USA and around the world.

http://www.earthquakes.com
The Global Earthquake Response Center is an American site full of reports and information on earthquakes from around the world.

http://tlc.discovery.com/tlcpages/greatquakes/ greatquakes.html
Check out the earthquake simulator and learn about the worst earthquakes this century.